JOURNAL OF EXPERIMENTAL FICTION

JEF

The First-Person Dilogy

●

Sebastian in a Dream

*a novel prompted by and written during the
time of the pandemic*

● ●

The Burial of the Count of Orgaz

*a novel prompted by and written during the
time of the war*

YURIY TARNAWSKY

SEBASTIAN IN A DREAM

a novel

2024

Cover Design by Norman Conquest
Author Photo by Yuriy Tarnawsky

ISBN 1-884097-13-8
ISBN-13 978-1-884097-13-3

ISSN 1084-547X

This is volume 100 of
The Journal of Experimental Fiction

JEF Books/Depth Charge Publishing
Arlington Heights, Illinois

JEF Books/Depth Charge Publishing
The Foremost in Innovative Fiction
Experimentalfiction.com

JEF Books and The Journal of Experimental fiction
are distributed to the academic market by EBSCO

Goldberg Variations *consists of thirty variations, preceded and followed by the same aria. The original and translation of Georg Trakl's poem is provided at the end of the text of the novel. A detailed account of the writing of* Sebastian in a Dream *can be found in Yuriy Tarnawsky's forthcoming JEF book* Literary Diary 2020-2024.

Mutter trug das Kindlein im weißen Mond
"Sebastian im Traum"
Greorg Trakl

Clavier Übung bestehend in einer ARIA
mit verschiedenen Verænderungen
vors Clavicimbal mit 2 Manualen.
Johann Sebastian Bach

DEAD STILL ALL around as in a tomb, am I in a tomb? dead? no, impossible, I'd be gasping, I mean, if I'm in a tomb, I'd be gasping if I were alive, otherwise I'd be dead, and I couldn't be dead because I'm thinking, you are, therefore you think, and if you think, you're alive, I don't believe in this crap of thinking in your grave, remembering, recollecting, it's not much better than "afterlife," sitting on a cloud and singing hymns to the Almighty, while bored angels mechanically strum their harps nearby, but where am I then that it's dead still all around as in a tomb? in a hospital? unlikely, there'd be equipment all over me, people around, I wouldn't be in a private room, don't warrant that, couldn't afford it, the stillness moreover feels different than in a single room, it's everywhere, all-penetrating, all-permeating, you don't have that kind of stillness in a hospital, there's something always going on there, people and all, I must be in a private house then most likely, my own, my home, why would I be lying in bed in somebody else's home? who would have me there? I have no friends, no real good friends who'd

Yuriy Tarnawsky

put me up in case of something, and there must be something with me, judging from the way I feel, something serious, perhaps grave, I must be in my own home then, almost certainly so, but where are the others, my wife, children? I did have a wife and children, didn't I? everybody does or almost everybody, it almost always depends on the person, and I'm not the kind of person who wouldn't have a family, I'm sure of that, I am a family kind of person, so I should have a family, but where are they momentarily? on an errand? unlikely, they wouldn't leave me all alone in the state I'm in, I'm also sure of that, and it's not as if it's been quiet in the house for just a few moments and the person who's there will stir and all of a sudden you'll know you're not alone, it's been still like this for a while, for a long time in fact, it's that kind of stillness, you can tell it by hearing it, it sounds different, so where are they all? did they all die? I seem to have attended a funeral recently, in fact I seem to have just returned from a funeral, but whose funeral? my wife's? one of my children's? all of them? that's unlikely, why unlikely? it's quite possible, in fact it's quite likely, happens all the time nowadays, a car accident or an act of terror, we were together, driving in a car or attending some event and were in a car crash or became victims of a terrorist attack respectively, all were hurt, the others died, and I am the only survivor, but no, that's not it, for one, I wouldn't be at home all alone and I'd feel different, bereaved and so on, but the feeling I have is not like that, not bereaved, but abandoned, all alone, abandoned on purpose, by design, according to plan, so there's something else going on here, still there was a funeral, I'm sure, in driving rain, on a hill, the coffin on a horse-drawn wagon or in a hearse, a car hearse, I mean, a black automobile hearse, shiny from the rain, wet, slippery, blinding-green grass underfoot so that I had to lean to one side, left, I think, yes, left, in order not to slide down and fall, dug the edges of my shoes into the ground to make sure, were all muddy when I got home and I had to wash them in the sink in the bathroom, had a kink in my side the next day for a week or two because of that, no, not because of leaning, because of getting wet on that side from the rain and getting a chill, yes, that's right, it was my right side, the one that was exposed to the rain because I was leaning to the left, tried to hide under a huge umbrella, big as the sky, as the vast black sky overhead, above it, but wasn't quite able to, the rain kept coming in, the umbrella, big as it was, strangely enough wasn't big enough, not big enough even though as big as the vast black sky overhead, the sky

Yuriy Tarnawsky

somehow bigger, the rain somehow managing to get under the umbrella, and the sky blacker even though the umbrella as black as the sky, no umbrella could be as black as the sky if you're attending a funeral, the sky black not from the clouds, the rain, but from the funeral, but I probably didn't have a kink just because of the umbrella being too small and my getting wet on one side either but because of both, because of both leaning and being wet, but that's another matter, but who was the funeral for? who had died? there was only one coffin, I am sure, I remember seeing it pitifully small and lonely, small and abandoned, on that wagon, or inside the hearse, no, it was a wagon after all, a simple horse-drawn wagon, pulled by one horse, one miserable-looking skinny old horse, and there was one coffin on it, so it must have been one person, one person who had died, who could it have been? my wife? a child? it wasn't a woman though, wife, or daughter, I know that, it was a man, so it could have been a son, I must have had one, yes, I remember now, I did, what was/is his name? wait, wait a second, it's on the tip of my tongue, wait, wait, no, I can't remember it right now, won't remember it anytime soon either, not in the state I'm in, not with the way I feel, but it'll come back, I'm sure, I just have to be patient and it'll come

4

back, so the funeral could have been for him and I was the only one there, the only mourner in addition to the gravedigger or gravediggers and the driver of the wagon or the hearse, don't remember how many, but why was I alone? where was my wife, his mother? I must have had a wife or a woman to have him with, and he of course did have a mother, did she die before him? no, I'm sure of that, I would have felt it then and would feel it now, but I don't know where she was, busy? what do I mean busy? how can you be too busy with something so that you wouldn't be able to attend your son's funeral? well, she may have been away, someplace far away on business and couldn't make it back in time, so I had to bury him alone, or maybe she abandoned him, abandoned both of us long time ago and didn't care what happened to him, hadn't been in touch with us for years, since his birth perhaps, or I didn't know how, or didn't want to get in touch with her to let her know our son had died because she had abandoned him and me long time ago, there could have been all sorts of reasons, anyway, there was no woman with me and I was there alone for the man who died, who may have been my son, but was it my son? I am not sure, that it was a man, I am sure, yes, but my son, no, not sure of that, so who could it have been? a friend? no,

Yuriy Tarnawsky

it wasn't a friend, it was someone very close to me, related, a brother? no, I never had a brother, an uncle, a relative? no, definitely not, it was someone very close, very, very close, as close as anybody can be, a son or father, so if it wasn't my son, then it must have been my father, yes, of course, it was my father, I remember now clearly, it was his funeral, we were the only two left of our family and when he died, I was the only one left to mourn him, it was some years ago though, I was still young then, but no, my father's funeral was different, there were many cars there, black, limousines, a flag leaning, grazing like a horse on the shiny funeral home tiled floor, and many people, I did have siblings, a brother and a sister, I remember now, and they were there, yes, for sure, so this was a different funeral, different from the one I've just attended, I'm all confused, was I actually at such a funeral as I've described? I'm not sure now, it's possible I'm just imagining, I may have read about it someplace and think now that it was I who attended it, by association, being in a similar situation, putting myself in that person's, the mourner's place, yes, I think so, it's quite possible that this is what happened, in fact I am almost sure now that that's what happened, that I have read someplace about such a funeral and in the state I'm in confused it with what I've lived through, probably through association, being in a similar situation, putting myself in that person's, the mourner's place, so it also means that I didn't attend any funeral recently as I have thought earlier, that I'm just back from one, which most likely means that my son hasn't died because I surely would remember it even in the state I'm in, the way I feel, that is, if I had him, if I ever had a son, but I must have had one, why would I have been punished in such a horrible way as to have been denied the gift of having a son? I hadn't done anything to deserve it, fate couldn't have been so cruel as to deny me that natural gift, so I probably have one and he's just away, went out on an errand, to do something important, to get something, for instance for himself, or for us both, medicine or food, or a special kind of drink, an electrolyte drink for me for instance, or for both of us, and will be back soon to attend to me, I must be patient, I must wait.

1

THERE'S A MAN standing in the doorway, I can see him if I move my eyes all the way to the right and turn my head on the pillow as far as I can, he's tall, slender, young, has long dark hair, neatly combed, it molds itself neatly around his nicely-shaped head, who is it? I don't seem to know him but on the other hand his face seems very familiar, it's as if we've spent a lot of time together, the name Sebastian pops up in my mind, it must be his name, it sounds so familiar, I must have known it for a long time, used it for a long time, weird, who could he be? my son? I never had a son, but who else would I have known for so long? I feel I've known him from his childhood, couldn't have been a friend, an acquaintance, he looks much younger than me, friendships and acquaintances aren't established at such an early age, so, a son? my son? but I never had a son, or did I? did I have a son? perhaps, perhaps I did and have forgotten, things like that happen, it could have happened if he left me long time ago and my memory of him has faded away with time, but,

9

Yuriy Tarnawsky

no, his name and face wouldn't seem so familiar, had he left me as a child, I wouldn't know what he looked like grown up, and his name wouldn't seem so familiar to me now, it would have faded away in my mind, unless I kept repeating it to myself all the time, missing him a lot, missing him immensely, loving him so much perhaps, but then why is his face so familiar to me? because I saw him in pictures? because he or someone else was sending them to me, maybe it was a recent one and I was looking at it all the time because I missed him a lot, loved him so much, but this is too farfetched, it doesn't make sense, although it's not impossible, not everything in life must make sense, farfetched things do happen, are possible, anyway, it appears he's most likely my son and has come to see me, because he loves me, because of my state, somebody must have told him about it, me, or maybe not, maybe we're living together and he was downstairs or in another room and has come in to check up on me, or more likely had gone out on an errand, to the bank or post office, or to get groceries at the supermarket, or something to drink, an electrolyte drink for me, for instance, it's dangerous if you lose them, the electrolytes, don't have enough of them, I must need it, a drink like that, in the state I'm in, with the stress I've been going through lately and the usual old-age nightmares and sweats, you lose electrolytes for sure, the same as exercising, or for both of us, that is, maybe he had gone out to get an electrolyte drink for both of us, young people exercise too much, undergo stress too and sweat, whatever, don't have enough of them, of the electrolytes, or maybe he had gone out to get something at the pharmacy, a prescription medicine, a prescription medicine for me most likely, and has come back and is checking up on me, to see how I'm doing, Sebastian! Sebastian! words don't seem to get out of my mouth, that is, they do but are not words but silence, air, empty air, vacuum, I speak vacuum, Sebastian! Sebastian! Stop! Stop! You're going to hurt yourself, you'll fall down! Stop! he giggles as if spilling handfuls of glass beads on the hard, bare, wood floor and runs as fast as he can on his stiff short little legs, bare-footed, stark naked, thud, thud, thud, thud, thud, down the long, empty bare-floored, bare-walled, dark hallway toward the light at the end coming in through the open door on the left, I chase after him, dive, catch him just before he falls down the stairs on the left, no, no stairs there, before he falls down flat on the hard, bare wood floor and hurts himself, like catching a football in the air just before it hits the ground and rolling with

Yuriy Tarnawsky

it on the grass, keeping it up so that it won't touch the ground, I hold him up by his hips, he was turning around just as I was catching him and giggles, I lay him down on the bare wood floor, lean over him, press my mouth to his soft warm little belly, blow, the skin, flesh makes a funny percolating sound, bbl-bbl-bbl-bbl, like thick liquid, liquid mud bubbling with air blowing up through it, he giggles, laughs, struggles, tries to free himself, I guess it tickles him, I go on and on, he continues, I'm beginning to have enough of this, slow down more and more, he quiets down proportionally, in the end we lie next to each other quiet on the hard floor, I panting, he breathing evenly, hard wood floor? bare? no, on something soft, a carpet, rug, captain's bed? the room not empty as I thought, a carpet, captain's bed on the right, a few more pieces in the corners, behind us, I caught him by the bed so that he wouldn't hurt himself on its hard corner and rolled on the carpet next to it together with him.

2

SO THE APARTMENT isn't empty, also there seems to be someone else living with us in it, a woman? a woman most probably, his mother? his mother most likely, who else? he must have or must have had a mother, everyone has or has had a mother, I couldn't have brought him into the world by myself, of course not, I didn't propose that, I mean I didn't propose that I'd adopted him alone, not being married, I don't think you can do that, they don't let you, but even if they do it's not the case here, I feel sure that if he's my son, I didn't adopt him, I had him with a woman, my wife? most likely my wife, or a woman who lives with us, which means a wife even if we're not officially married, his mother, she must be away now, perhaps she's at work and that's why we're alone, it would make sense, she works and I take care of our son, I must have lost my job, am unemployed, unemployable, don't want to work, so she has to work to support us, it makes sense, things like that happen nowadays, are common, yes, and I may not want to work because I want to take care of

13

him, because I love him so much, because he means so much to me, and my wife agreed to work instead of me to make me happy, because she loves me so much, because she loves both of us a lot and knows that I would take good care of him, as good as anyone or better, including herself, strange, but I don't recall who she is, have no idea who she is or looks like, except, wait, I seem to remember walking next to a woman, a young woman, almost a girl through darkness, night, she holding up her pregnant belly with her hands, arms, white, both hands/arms and belly white like the huge full white moon up in the sky above us, she clearly naked, me, I think too, among trees, yes, among trees because it's dark sometimes, dark in places, that is, dark when we're in the shadow of a tree, whereas it's clear nearly as in the daytime otherwise, walking naked, through woods, in the middle of the night, under full moon? isn't that weird? it sure is weird, couldn't have happened, of course it could have, all sorts of weird crazy things happen in life and that's why it's interesting, wonderful, that's why everyone wants to stay alive, live, hoping for some strange wonderful thing to happen to them because if everything in life were commonplace, predictable who would want to live, go on, you'd go crazy with boredom, commit suicide, there'd be people hanging down from trees everywhere, all over, strange low-hanging rotting fruit, for instance, us walking like that together could have been part of some ritual, an old folk ritual that has been revived, perhaps having to do with fertility, I seem to feel there's a huge river somewhere nearby there, on the left, we're high up on a ridge, hill, hills, in the woods that grow over them, and there's a huge river on the left below, perhaps we're walking down to it for her or both of us to bathe in it, it's flat where we're walking but we might be following a path that further along turns left and descends and so we are heading for the river, I think that fertility rights for some peoples did involve rivers, water, bathing in it, but she's pregnant already, so that doesn't make sense, but no, it's possible, maybe she had trouble conceiving, and we followed this ritual, say a year ago, and now that it was successful, we've come back to conclude it, pay our homage to the deity that's helped her to get pregnant, maybe it's a holiday devoted to that deity during a particular day of the year and we've come to pay homage to it and make sure the pregnancy will end successfully, her belly is really huge, so maybe the baby's overdue and we're trying to make sure it'll be born healthy, it might be the midsummer night for instance, the shortest night of the year, which I think had great significance among certain ethnic groups in the old times and therefore might still have now, which would make it likely that fertility rituals would be conducted in the course of it, it feels in fact like it's during that time of the year, that of his mother and me walking through the woods naked in the middle of the night under a full moon, her belly so huge she had to hold it up with both her hands, it must have been part of that ritual, probably to ask the deity for the child, our son to be born healthy, he must have been way overdue so we worried he, it, the child, might be born abnormal, a mooncalf, with a huge head, water on his brain, retarded, but he, the man in the doorway, he's not retarded, he looks normal, looks very normal, almost abnormally normal, abnormally well-formed, well-proportioned and handsome, but there was a retarded child, a little boy with Down Syndrome, where we lived at the time, son of the caretaker, the one who lived in an apartment in the basement, he, the boy would run around in the asphalt-covered court within the apartment complex on his short, stiff little legs, shouting, Huh, huh, huh, huh, huh! all the time, stabbing with his short little finger in all directions as his father was sweeping up the place with his huge birch-branch broom, he, the boy was called Sebastian, I recall his father speaking to him gently,

No, Sebastian, no Sebastian, you can't do that, Sebastian, and sometimes shouting, No, Sebastian, no! but was it perhaps him, that is, my son and me? in other words, is it possible that the little boy was Sebastian and I his father? meaning that our son was born retarded after all, after all that pleading and all the rituals? we living in a basement apartment and I being a caretaker, sweeping up courtyards with a birch-branch broom? ridiculous! impossible! I never swept up anything with a birch-branch broom nor anything else and never lived in a basement apartment! I'm sure of that, sure as I can be sure of anything, hmmm, that is, I'm not sure, but only hope and think it's untrue, you can never be sure of anything, all sort of impossible things are possible in life, but it's very likely untrue, that is, it's most, most unlikely, but if it's untrue, if our son is normal, then why did we call him Sebastian, with a little Down Syndrome boy named Sebastian running around outside the widows and his father calling out his name all the time? we certainly didn't name him after the little boy, or did we? so as to make up for the fact he was retarded? but that doesn't make sense, how would we have made up for his shortcomings? it wouldn't have made him less retarded, no, it's impossible, that is, it's very, very, most, most unlikely, but wasn't it strange then for us to call our son the same as the little retarded boy? wouldn't it have bothered us? unless we did it earlier, that is, unless our son was born earlier and we named him Sebastian before we moved into that apartment, but we also could have done it even while living there, loving the name so much that we weren't bothered by a Down Syndrome Sebastian running around outside our windows, Sebastian is such a beautiful name, why should we have cared? why would the fact there was a retarded boy who was named Sebastian living in an apartment below had prevented us from naming our son Sebastian? we loved the name and decided to call our son by it, that's all, it's that simple.

3

BUT WHY? WHY would we have liked the name so much? why is it so beautiful for me? because of the saint? no, definitely not! I wouldn't associate my son with that androgynous figure with its white effeminate body stuck full of arrows, looking like a seamstress' pincushion full of needles, standing meekly against the tree, Bach then? Johann SEBASTIAN? hmmm, I really love Bach's music but somehow I don't think I would have named my son Sebastian after him, Bach is Johann Sebastian to me and I think of him as this prickly, fractious, somewhat rotund individual with a full, Newt Gingrich face, sporting an epee on his belt, walking down Leipzig sidewalks, picking fights with passers-by, completely unlike the image of a Sebastian I have in my mind, no, that's not it, there seems to be something in the name itself, the way it sounds, that makes me like it, Se-ba-sti-an, e-a-i-a, these four open vowels, the way they go together, open up into vast spaces filled with light, freedom, future, but wait! wasn't there a horse? a beautiful Arab stallion belonging to the count on whose estate we lived when I was little named Sebastian? he had a shimmering milk-white body, a long muscular neck with a tiny head on the end like the scroll on a fine old Italian violin that didn't seem to belong there but looked beautiful, thin graceful legs, and small shiny porcelain-cup-like hoofs his white body was poured into? he'd run around all day in the corral, jumping up and kicking up his hind feet way high and then plunging down to the ground head first like a dolphin frolicking in sea waves, full of himself, admiring himself in his movements like Narcissus in the water of the spring, god, no! that's not true! he wasn't called Sebastian but Narcissus, I think precisely because of that, because of being so much in love with himself, and was coal-black, looking as I described him but black, I think he was actually called Black Narcissus, although people referred to him as Narcissus because it was simpler, no, the name Sebastian definitely wouldn't have fit him, but wait again! wait! open spaces filled with light, freedom, future, yes! I think this time I've got it! I have an image of a man, young, good-looking, with dark hair, a smooth oval face, and a swarthy complexion sitting at a table next to the wall of a house outside, drinking a glass of rose wine, my God, yes! that's it! and it's me! it's not a picture but my memory, as I remember, imagine myself sitting outside in the backyard of that first house I bought, the day I moved in, I brought out a table and a chair, put them down close to the house, sat down, and drank a bottle of semi-sparkling Portuguese rose wine, Lancers, I think it was called, yes, Lancers, I felt so wonderful, young, strong, healthy, with a potentially glorious future stretching before me, mine for the taking! god, how I wish I was there right now, looking like that, being what I was then instead of being where I am and what I am now! so that's why I like that name so much! I associate it with myself, with my being young, and I wanted to name my son by that name, to make him myself, to continue myself in him, yes, of course, what's so strange about that? this is what everyone does with their children, but no, that's not true here, with me it's different, I didn't want him just to carry on my name or even my genes, but to be me, and me to be him, I wanted to be father and son, son and father at the same time, that's what I wanted! that's why I named him Sebastian! that's why! but maybe not, maybe I wasn't influenced by anything particular and just dreamed it, or maybe hadn't even dreamt it and only wish I had, am dreaming the whole thing up from nothing, maybe I don't exist, Sebastian! Sebastian! silence, no reply.

4

I TURN MY head right, move my eyes, look, and he's not there, has gone away, just looked in, saw I was quiet, and went away, has other things to do, bigger fish to fry, his own, that matter more than my wellbeing, matters of the heart and the crotch, mostly the crotch, I'm sure, closer to crotch than to heart, my not stirring doesn't mean I'm fine, I could be dead, he didn't care to check, if he had really cared, he'd have checked or at least asked if I was fine, kids are like that, everyone is, I was this way with my father, so he, I mean life is paying me back now, I have earned it, I deserve it, but maybe he did check, spoke to me, asked me if I was fine, I said, I was, he helped me to be more comfortable, and went away, maybe to get me something, a drink of water, or lemonade, or tea, maybe I'd asked him, my head's in a different position now, higher up, I was looking straight forward before I turned my head, so maybe that's what happened, yes, I seem to remember him coming up to the bed, asking me how I feel, helping me sit up, and

Yuriy Tarnawsky

going downstairs to fix me a drink, I think I told him I was thirsty and he suggested he'd fix me a glass of lemonade, I like lemonade, my mother used to fix it for me when I was sick as a child, the usual childhood fevers, sweats, like he used to have when he was little and I'd fix lemonade for him, lukewarm, I liked it better that way when little and so did he, it goes into your system faster, I think, so that's what he must be doing now, no, that's not true, he wasn't here, I think I got up alone a short while back to relieve myself in the bathroom, feel comfortable now, didn't before, that's all, he's probably out on an errand, trying to get me something, the house all quiet, empty, still as a tomb, that sick, perverted, selfish, lying bitch, made his body bounce off the bare walls like an echo in the empty rooms, his mouth spew not screams but giant jets of black smoke, call his lawyer, father for help in the cadaver-gray pre-dawn dusk, he having tossed around all night in his bed like a weird live stone in a dry riverbed possessed by an evil energy, a sudden, unexpected, frightening void in his mind where the huge sharp-edged diamond of love had been painfully embedded for sixteen years, what to do, where to go? no roads, paths ahead, just a vast plain of gravel and boulders, no wall behind, no bottomless precipice, but simply nothing you can't even think your way into let alone step, but the only way is forward and that is where you will step, he? it wasn't he but me, of course, the end of that great love of mine, he never made it that far in life, no! I lost him! his white body came back from that crazy war in the east riddled with bullets, a veritable sieve, a modern-day Sebastian, one of our times, pierced by contemporary arrows, the arrows of our times, brass machine-gun slugs, not a pincushion, a sieve, I shouldn't have named him Sebastian, or did I name him Sebastian after his body came back, to fit the image of his white body riddled with bullets? yes, I did, I renamed him, I'd named him originally something else, so that he wouldn't die like that, like that saint, pierced all over by something, so that he'd live to a ripe old age, but that didn't work, yes it did, it did! I mean, no, I didn't name him something else, I did name him Sebastian, but that body that came back wasn't his, he came back alive, that is, he never went to that war, it was Seb, Sebastian Soriano, our neighbors' Sorianos' son, who came back riddled with bullets, looking like a sieve, people said they shouldn't have named their son Sebastian, they were tempting their fate, they themselves said, Had we named him something else he might still be alive, it's our fault, they must have thought it was our fault too because they named their son Sebastian after ours, after we'd moved into the neighborhood and we became friends, but they never said so, he was born about a year after we came and they named him Sebastian because they liked the name as well as our son, they wanted their son to be like ours, were nice people, of Spanish origin, apparently originally from Soria, where Antonio, Antonio Machado, he himself says, spent twenty years of his youth, I think he met, married, and buried his wife there, never got over the loss, who would if you love the person? part of your life, yourself, who wouldn't mourn part of yourself passing? that's why I mourn him to this day, every day, after all these years, part of myself, more than part of myself! all of myself! me! god, no! what am I saying again? I'm asking for trouble, he didn't die! it was Seb Soriano who did and we're not Sorianos, he's alive! he stands there in the doorway, has just come back, he's done with his errands and has come to check up on me, in fact he's just come up right now and stands by the bed, you want to hear the story? the one about the girl Flamina, who's woken up every night just as she's falling asleep by the little bird that sits down on the windowsill of her bedroom window by going, Ping! like a little gold bell, and she wakes up immediately, and steps out into the garden, and climbs over the fence, and finds there in the purling brook that streams by a silver boat with a golden oar, and gets into the boat, and starts rowing, and travels down the brook into the sea on the bottom of which there is another world, bright in the sunlight because it's daytime there, a world with hills, and valleys, and forests, and fields, and roads cutting through the latter, and hamlets, and villages, and towns with big houses in them with steep red-tiled roofs, and churches with tall spires, and streets and squares between them, and people like tiny black ants moving around in them, busy with their daily chores, and there's a big beautiful sail ship with its three sails furled up ahead where the boy Flamino is waiting for her, and she rows to it very quickly but without any effort because the water in that sea makes it easy for one to row, as easy as skating on ice, like skating on canals in the old times in Holland when winters were long and hard, and Flamino helps her to climb up onto the ship and welcomes her by kissing her on both cheeks, while she kisses him back, and he's dressed in a loose white shirt with puffy sleeves, and tight green satin pants, and tall boots of yellow Morocco leather on his feet, and her nightshirt by then has changed into a beautiful long lavender silk dress and she's wearing gold slippers on her feet whereas she was barefoot when climbed out the window, and Flamino unfastens the ropes on the three masts and the sails immediately fill up with wind and look like three giant white swans anxious to go, and the ship takes off real fast and very soon arrives at The Magic Island, which has changed its form since they were there last, having gotten narrower but longer and taller in the middle, and the boat moors itself in the harbor by itself, and they're welcomed by The Good Fairy who's dressed in a long pale blue silk dress that covers her feet and a tall white conical hat on her head with a white veil on it that covers her face, holding in her hand her golden magic wand with a huge diamond on the end, who's come to greet them with her suite of servants and musicians who play lutes, and fifes, and one or two tambourines struck gently from time to time, and The Good Fairy's huge palace with its many windows and terraces stands on the hill behind her, overlooking a beautiful formal garden with hedges and roses and white sand paths between them, a palace in which there are rooms where you can enter different worlds, worlds that are pink, and blue, and yellow, and upside down, and so on, and she greets them by saying, Welcome to The Magic Island, children! and by also kissing each of them on both cheeks after she lifts up her veil, and they in turn kiss her, and it's hot in the bright sunshine, and the air is heavy with the smell of roses, and you can hear insects buzzing all around, and there are two beautiful bay horses being held by servants, moving nervously around in one spot and snorting impatiently, ready to go, and Flamino and Flamina step up to them, and are helped into their saddles, Flamina's being one for ladies, on which you sit sideways, and they ride off into the forest on the hill before them, with the musicians following them for a little while, but then they find themselves alone in the dark woods, with huge, tall trees towering over them, riding along a path that winds its way between them which the horses know on their own, having travelled it many times, and after a while they find themselves in a clearing with their beautiful little stone house with a gray slate roof surrounded by a garden full of fruit trees and roses in it waiting all ready for them, you want to hear the story? no? you don't want to hear it? you've heard it many times before? have enough of it? no? why don't you want to hear it then? why not? why? why?

5

WHY, YOU SONOFABITCH of a freak, locked up there in your shabby one-room attic apartment so that no one sees you, you evil humpbacked dwarf with an over-acid stomach burning up your insides from an inexplicable hatred, stinking up with your sour breath the air around you, the whole universe, why do you prevent a person from having someone to tell a little fairytale about a boy and a girl being happy on an island that changes its shape? they don't do anything bad there, the person in question hasn't done anything bad either, so why can't he or she have somebody to tell that story to? it's just a sweet little lie, a silly little tale about how life could be different from ours, full of exciting promises and possibilities, it doesn't hurt anyone, doesn't cause any harm, and only brings the person a little bit of joy, so, why, can't you let him or her have that little pleasure? why, you sonofabitch, why? but that's nothing, I mean it's just a drop, no, a molecule, an atom, part of an atom, an electron, neutron, proton, whatever, in the ocean, an ocean of flesh and lives, of people's biographies, I think I know someone, someone close to me, a boy I think I know real well but at this moment for some reason can't remember who, who at the age of ten lost his mother and father and was left alone in a hostile foreign country to fend for himself, so why did you do that to him? he hadn't done anything bad to anyone except for drowning a kitten or two at somebody's request and catching some fish to bring home for supper, for how could he have done something really bad at his age? and his parents hadn't done anything bad either, and even if they did, why would you punish their child for their deeds? even the most vicious regimes, repressive societies don't do that, so why would you, you, the fairest of the fair would do that to him? why, you sonofabitch, why? but that's nothing again, or almost nothing, I remember that beggar girl or woman, I couldn't tell which, she was so deformed, I saw once on the sidewalk in Mérida, Mexico, covered with a pile of rags, reaching her hand out for alms, for a few centavos, skinnier than skinny, a bunch of bones shoved in helter-skelter into the dark brown, nearly black leather sack of her skin, her spine was so compressed that with her sitting up, her chin almost rested on the sidewalk, no, what am I saying? not her chin, her jaw, her upper jaw was resting on the sidewalk, the lower one being under it, the only normal, undeformed part of her were her eyes, huge, brown, frightening, staring at me, asking, why, why did this happen to me? what did I do to deserve this? I was born this way, so what am I being punished for? what monstrous sin that would warrant such a punishment did I commit while being still in my mother's womb? so, why did you, you sonofabitch, do that to her? what is that evil, that hatred inside you that causes you do such things? what made you this way? what did they do to you that you've turned out to be like this? you're the almighty one, the creator, right? so you could do anything, could right any wrong, could make it so that there isn't any wrong in the world, so why is it not like that? or is the almighty part a lie, and there are things you can't do? I seem to feel I have read someone say someplace that you are a paralytic, a quadriplegic, or higher than quadri-, centi-, milli, whatever -plegic, of cosmic dimensions, as big as the world, the cosmos, unable to stir, do anything, and that you are kept alive by being fed by bees and comets, and that butterflies settle on you and move their wings to keep you cool, and fishes nibble at your skin and rub against it with their bodies to ease the pain in your paralyzed body, but only minutes, no, literary seconds, probably no more than ninety

seconds, that is a minute and a half after I saw that woman/
girl-lower-jaw-under-the-sidewalk creature, some fifty yards
away, along the street that ran along the little park
perpendicular to the one in question, I ran into the beautiful
blue-eyed Susan, right one after the other, almost together,
the ugliest and the prettiest at the same time for comparison,
as if he was flaunting his might, his evil nature, saying,
here's what I can do, see? I could have made both of them
beauties but chose this one to be a freak because it pleased
me, for no other reason, just because it pleased me, see? I
could have gone the other way too but didn't, see? that's all,
you see? I met her, the blue-eyed Susan, a day or two
before, no, the day before for sure, I remember now because
I couldn't get her out of my mind and kept hoping, praying
every second I'd run into her and couldn't have lasted two
days like that without her, it was at the blue Xel-Ha lagoon,
blue as her blue-Texas-sky eyes, on the bus trip back from
Palenque, during a stopover, and I went bathing and took a
picture of her and sent it to her later, Susan Crow, Snow?
can't remember, couldn't have been Crow for she was too
beautiful, nor Snow either, Snow means cold, winter and she
sure wasn't winter, spring rather, the beautiful warm month
of May, Susan May, that would have been appropriate,

Susan May, let's say she was called Susan May, I think she was twenty-two then, I was going to that restaurant I used to go to all the time to gorge myself on *pan y salsa cruda* you could have your heart's, stomach's full with the beer you drank, cold, frothy, refreshing in the heavy, oppressive, wet heat, I think she'd just stepped out of it, was with the three friends I saw her with at Xel-Ha, and she was all smiles and the blue sapphire eyes sparkling, sending off showers of bright sparks like Christmas tree sparklers, and said she was surprised, glad to see me, and reminded me of the picture I took and asked to be sure and send it to her, to the address I'd written down which I said I of course would, and then, still smiling and sending off sparks, asked if I could loan her two dollars because she needed them to pay the airport exit tax with because she was leaving that afternoon and had run out of money, she would pay them back to me as soon as she got home, send them to the address I'd given her, and I lit up all inside, and turned subservient as if before a great authority, and said I certainly would, and that it would bring me great pleasure, and that she didn't have to pay them back to me, and took out my wallet and looked inside, I had in fact two one-dollar bills and also a few five-dollar ones and tens and twenties, and told her I could give her five, or ten, or

35

twenty, but she said, no, two was enough, so, disappointed, I took the two one-dollar bills out and gave them to her, and she took them and smiled and thanked me, her face and eyes were so close, and I bent down and kissed her, probing her lips with my tongue, and between them her tongue responded, wiggling bashfully, tickling mine, made me imagine penetrating between her majora and minora and finding the remnants of her hymen blocking my way, I don't think, that beautiful, she could have been still a virgin, the three friends were gone by then, not gone, standing at the street corner, some ten yards away, waiting discreetly for her to join them after we were finished, what happened to us? did we see each other again? became lovers? got married? strange, but I don't remember? probably nothing happened, we probably never saw each other again, the only thing I remember is that one dark rainy night, as I lay in bed alone in the huge empty house writhing in the throes of solitude because she hadn't called me for a while, as I tried to visualize her face and kept saying, Call, please call, please call! at the instant her face was about to come into view, the phone rang, and it was her, it was windy there too and the branches of the tree outside her window were knocking on her pane as never before and she realized it was high time she called.

6

Alone as years, decades earlier, as I lay on that caved-in hunchbacked mattress on the squeaky iron bed, don't remember if with a bedside table next to it or not, a scratched-up plain wooden one against one wall, a ditto chair next to it, a scuffed-up wooden chest of drawers against another, a faded mirror in a ditto frame above it, grayness instead of daylight pushing its way inside through the narrow window caked up with a layer of dirt on the outside, in that furnished room in a plain bleak brick house, a real bleak house on a bleak treeless street lined with other plain bleak brick houses on both sides as far as the eye could see in both directions, in that furnished room I rented when I got my first job, I mean my first professional job, after finishing college, not counting those I had while working my way through school, summers on assembly line, working nightshift at a beer can company, cut my leg on a sharp piece of sheet metal clearing a jam on the conveyor belt one day, I mean night, and nearly bled to death, sleep-walked in

Yuriy Tarnawsky

the daytime once from exhaustion, found myself locked out
on the staircase landing clad in my skivvies, shorts, no one
at home in the daytime, so had to creep along the facade
holding on to the wall to get back in through the window,
luckily open, to wild *piropos,* whistles from the street below,
elevator operator nights at school during the schoolyear
Monday through Thursday, six to eight, and eight hours
Saturdays as a shipping clerk at a tannery, measuring skins,
packing, and sending them out, white privilege, you know,
privilege to work yourself to death, it got me far, this far, all
the way to this cold lonely bed, so when I got my first full-
time, professional job, having moved to another town, a
small town in the middle of nowhere, far away from
everything and everyone, stretched out on my back on the
bed in my room, fully dressed, shirt, pants, shoes on, too
tired, depressed to take them off, the stuffy air like a heavy
smelly sweat-soaked pillow pressed tight over my face,
making it hard for me to breathe, sweat standing out on,
trickling down my face, first the upper lip, then the forehead,
then the rest of the face, running down the cheeks onto the
jaws, then the neck, creeping along in the back, tickling me,
forcing me to finally move, wipe it off, nibbling on my skin like
worms will be nibbling one day on my flesh in my coffin, a

training session for being dead, lying in my grave, loneliness together with heat streaming out of the dark red-roses-on-brown-background wallpapered walls like a faint high-pitched whining sound coming out of a turned-down radio, after work, from dinner at the cafeteria at one of the company's manufacturing facilities open in the evening for employees working the nightshift, the food not bad, prices too, but most importantly the company of colleagues from work, other lonely ones like me, almost like at home at my father's, or direct from the office when it seemed even company of other lonelies wouldn't help, but later lonely in a different way when I moved to that cozy room in the second floor apartment owned by the two spinsters one of whom died when I was there and lay comfortable on the dining room table tucked in among white lilies or whatever those flowers were, and the one that was left tried to force my hand onto those of the dead one folded, crossed on her abdomen which I desperately and successfully resisted as she kept pressing it down, a room furnished in Victorian style, packed chuck-full like a store with carved curly-cued dark-wood furniture, with walls like flower gardens left untended, overgrown with peonies, and roses, and god knows what other imaginary Victorian flowers, a room with breakfast of

Yuriy Tarnawsky

tea, toast, and two soft-boiled eggs in the morning, and I got myself a record player like a small square gray suitcase and my first record, Bach's sonatas and partitas for solo violin, and would play it over and over, the player on the floor in the corner, I once again lying stretched out fully dressed but with my shoes off on the now soft comfortable bed, after walking seven blocks back from the luncheonette I for some reason fell in love with where I had every night a bowl of chicken alphabet soup out of a can and a cheeseburger so that eventually my gums started bleeding until someone explained to me what was happening and I began adding fresh fruit and some vegetables to my diet at the cafeteria at work, this time loneliness not streaming in from the outside but generated, produced inside me and the music, first the sonata, Sonata No. 1 in G-major, and then the partita, Partita No. 2 in D-minor, especially the second and in particular its Chaconne, the twenty-nine variations, fifteen in D-minor, nine in D-major, and five in D-minor again, that is the violin, describing and explaining it to me like a clear calm voice of an expert, telling me what and why I felt as I did, I lying spellbound, unable to move, mesmerized by what I heard, its beauty, clarity, logic, see, this is what you feel, and this, and this, and this, and this is why you feel it, and this, and this, and this, and this is how it fits into the rest of the world, like this, and like this, and like this, accept it, accept it because you're a man, a human being, as everyone else you are destined to be alone, you were born alone and will always be alone, even when you're jumping up and down with joy on the dance floor in the company of others, until that final moment when only you are there and you know that only you can be there and you make your exit, lying like that and listening night after night, for months, years, maybe decades, no, definitely not for decades and not for years either, actually only for about a dozen or so weeks, three or four months as I recall, until the fall, when I got myself an apartment, a dining alcove, living room, bedroom, kitchen, bathroom, and a long dark hallway, there the loneliness different, loneliness of empty space, of beaten up used furniture I purchased, of a round table with two folding wings and a chair in the alcove, of an aluminum folding cot with a thin mattress pallet for a couch in the living room, of a big old double bed, its footboard loose, in the bedroom with a stack of books on the floor on the right next to it for a night table, a beer bottle as a lamp base with a light bulb screwed into it on top, of a mustard-colored metal-topped table with wooden legs, no chair in the kitchen, of the telephone on the floor in

Yuriy Tarnawsky

the dark hallway, loneliness of white morgue-color walls, of floors painted blood red with the cracks between the thin slats intersecting like parallel lines at infinity that can never be reached, loneliness of a near-empty refrigerator with only a jar of pickles and of mustard and a plastic bag with sliced commercial rye bread in it, of breakfast consumed because of being rushed while standing up and looking out the window consisting of a slice of that bread with a thick layer of mustard spread over it with my finger, which I later licked off, and sips of hot boiled water drunk directly out of the spout of the kettle, in which it was boiled, because of not having yet bought myself a knife, and tea, and something to brew it in, and a cup from which to drink it, the effect this produced being as if I saw a tall wide yellow-brown brick wall collapsing on the other side of the street although there was no building there and I was seeing only a big maple tree whose leaves had barely started to turn yellow, at night I would walk ten blocks through a carefully selected network of tree-shaded streets to a movie theater called Juliette which stood on the corner across the street from the gate leading to the park-like campus of that famous girls' college, a Romeo set not on finding his Juliette, but to see what foreign movies would be playing in the coming days, to hitch up with the shadows of himself trembling on the slack surface of the movie screen.

7

A HUGE EMPTY house, it seems it's no longer empty, I think I hear noises coming from downstairs, he must have returned, will come up soon, step up closer to the bed so that you can hear me, do you want to hear about Flamino and Flamina sitting on their horses on the edge of the wood, she playing the lute and narrating how the four gnomes, Romo, Roro, Momo, and Moro and their brave little mushroom friend Ero are fighting the big stupid sixteen-legged dragon Black Tooth? yes? and how the four of them are woken up at night in their home by the sound, swoosh, swoosh, swoosh, swoosh coming from under their open window, making Romo sit up and listen carefully, and next Roro, followed by Momo, followed by Moro, each of the last three asking in a whisper, Who is it? on waking up and each most recently awoken one answering in turn in a whisper upon being asked, Somebody, because it is Somebody and he is digging a hole for them to go through to visit one of the strange worlds that are under the ground, and after the noises stop and they know the way for them is open, they sneak out of the house and go to the hole, and go down the stairs they find there into a strange world, upside down from ours, with different colors, where the sky may be green and the sea pink, and palm trees may have red trunks and blue fronds on top, and fish in the sea are transparent with precision Swiss clock mechanisms inside them, and birds are holes which flap their wings, and it is difficult for the gnomes to move there at first, being upside down, but they get used to it quickly, they are quick learners, and it will be difficult for them to move for a while when they come back because then everything will be upside down for them here? yes? yes, good, no, it's too early for stories, they need darkness, and you feeling sleepy, I'll tell it to you at night before you go to bed, or the one about the little dragon called li whose mother's name was liii and father's liiiiiiiii, because he was very, very big, who was pure white and one winter went out and got lost in the snow and couldn't find himself because the snow was the same color as he and he had to stay there until springtime when the snow melted, and his father liiiiiiiii was a great hunter who liked to hunt pots of sauerkraut soup, and would bag three or four or more big ones each time and would bring them home for his wife to warm up and they would have them for three or four nights in a row or more, they always tasted delicious because Iii was an excellent warmer-upper, so I will tell one of them to you at night, alright? yes, so let's play now hide and seek, alright? first you will count to ten and I will hide before you're finished and then you will look for me, and when you find me, I will count to ten and you will hide and I will look for you, no, you're too small for that, you can't count to ten yet, maybe three, wah, dah, de, or wah, de, dah, so how about exercising? we can do that, daddy will do pushups and you will count, alright? no, of course we can't because you can't count beyond two or three and daddy will do many pushups, a hundred, more, two hundred or even more, maybe two hundred and fifty, so we'll both do pushups, side by side, daddy and you, and we'll see who does more, alright? OK, here we go, one, two, three, four, five, six, seven, Sebastian, you're not next to me, are you doing pushups? where are you? Sebastian! Sebastian! where did you go? did you go hide someplace? we're not doing hide-and-seek, we're doing pushups, Sebastian! Sebastian! you're such a pain! now I have to go look for you, alright, where did you hide? in my room? behind the big secretary, no, you're not there, in the closet? the big one? no, the little one? no, Sebastian!

Yuriy Tarnawsky

you must be in one of the closets, you like them the most, that's where you usually go and hide among the clothes, Sebastian, do you know how many closets there are in the house? forty, I think, no, that's windows, I think there are forty-seven of them, we have fourteen closets, or maybe seventeen, now I have to go and look in all of them, all over the house, what a pain! no, I won't look over the whole house, just on this floor, I don't think he went downstairs or to the attic, I would have heard him, so I'll just look on this floor, in the closets and other places he likes, like under beds and in the corners, behind furniture or doors, oh, god! Sebastian, where are you? so many stupid closets, all narrow and dark, better to have fewer big ones, open, walk-in ones, they used to think differently back in the old days, when the house was built, also didn't have so many clothes, a good suit for Sunday, going to church and holidays, and a couple for during the week, for going to work, not like now, dozens of the one and the other and when there's no room, into storage, just in case, in a box and under the bed, for kids to hide behind, no, he's not there, Sebastian, where the hell are you?! he's not downstairs I'm sure, because I would have heard him going down, so he must be in his room, where we, I mean, I was doing pushups, in the closet, because there's no other place to hide there, the corners are open, his bed is too high, and the other one is a captain's bed, he couldn't have climbed into one of the drawers, I should have heard him go into the closet, but maybe he did it so softly I just didn't, because of doing the pushups, it's hard to hear when you're exerting yourself, the pressure in the veins somehow blocks the hearing, the eustachian tubes, I guess, cuts it off, it happens all the time with me at least, his climbing down the stairs would have been different, at least longer, I would have heard it, alright, Sebastian, I finally got you, come out! I know you're there! you couldn't be anywhere else, I'm opening the door, Sebastian?! goddamit! he's not there, where could he be? I'm not going to look for him all over this huge house, knowing he's not there, nor in the drawers, crazy! why am I doing this? he's not anywhere, he doesn't exist, and never did, it's not true! what am I saying? I'm asking for trouble, I'll make it true if I go on like this, Sebastian, did you get the things? good, everything? oranges, and persimmon tea, and Perrier, and lime to put a slice of it in it? great, I love the way it, that is, the way carbonated water seethes and complains when you throw something into it in a glass, like a slice of lime or lemon, or an ice cube or two, for a couple of seconds, just

Yuriy Tarnawsky

like a grumpy person grunting or mumbling something to himself or herself in reaction to something you've done he or she doesn't like but not going any further, too polite or kind to act obnoxious, just a bit of superficial, harmless, neurotic grumpiness, but sheer kindness and good nature underneath, do you remember that time in Rome in a café on Via Veneto, as we sat in the big, comfortable wicker chairs at a table, the place all empty and the rows and columns of empty chairs and tables spilling out of the dark interior onto the sidewalk like entrails out of the cut-open belly of a huge animal, a cow or bull or something, with the silent crowd like a flooded river carrying all sorts of things running by, that is the street, Via Veneto, like a river at high flood carrying the crowd along like tree trunks, and fragments of homes, and items of furniture such as wardrobes, and chests of drawers, and whatever else on its back, and the two of us sitting in the big comfortable wicker chairs and drinking Perrier or whatever that Italian mineral water is called, San Pellegrino, yes, it must have been San Pellegrino, it was in Italy, out of tall glasses, relaxing after having spent most of the day, sightseeing, the archeological sites, the Forum, and the Coliseum, and the Vatican, Sistine Chapel, and whatever else, or maybe something all dug up, a big mess, a *pasticciaccio brutto* on the Via Merulana, or maybe not, I remember I took a sip out of the glass and the water seethed in it as if saying, Stop bothering me! Can't you leave me alone for a moment? What a pest you are! God! or maybe it was you who took that sip and I heard the sound? do you remember? no? why would you? no one remembers little things like that except me, but, no, maybe it was neither me nor you but another person who took that sip, I remember now there was a man sitting with us and we were talking about making a movie, maybe it was him, he was a movie director and we were speaking about casting a particular role, who would be the best in it? do you remember? no? maybe you're right, maybe I just read about it somewhere and we were never there.

8

SHE TURNED AROUND and ran as fast as her legs would carry her past that famous cast iron fountain that whispers day in and day out soothing words in its lisping water language to the door leading to the underworld, the underground, and down the escalator to the subway station sixty or whatever it is yards below, no, no, why am I doing this again? why am I saying this? it wasn't her, but me, it was not she, but I who turned around and ran like crazy to the door, leading to the subway station way below and then down the moving escalator steps, nearly falling a few times and breaking my neck and being carried all the way to the platform to be deposited there like a limp full suit, after, that is, turning around and running away after taking her face in my hands and pressing my lips to hers, the coolness of her saliva just inside like a waft of fresh breeze blowing into my closed space, into the tightly closed space that was me, its, the saliva's taste, the very essence, the soul of grass, scaring me, god, what have I done? what am I doing? she's

Yuriy Tarnawsky

innocent, innocent, may never have been kissed, what will she do? scream? slap my face? call for help? call the police? shame! scandal! heard nothing, not a sound, word, went home, to my apartment, sixteen bare walls, factually not all bare but effectively yes, hard and impenetrable for sure, four tall ceilings, four parquet floors, single or groups of autistic deaf-mute items of furniture here and there, she was leaving the next morning, I sat down and penned a letter, confessed, pleading guilty, begged leniency, forgiveness, addressed it to her, her parents' home, which is where she was going, went outside, it was dark already, streets empty except for the scrawny haystacks of light under the street lamps, dropped it, the letter, in a nearby mailbox to make sure it'd make the morning pickup, and then what? nothing? never seen or heard from again? forget now, don't remember, somehow no, somehow alright, somehow letters and calls, telephone calls probably, probably declarations of love, confessions, I fell in love with you the moment I first saw you, admissions of joy, plans, plans for the future, the near future, impatience, anticipations, descriptions of impending joy, and yes, I waiting on the train platform three or four months later, in September, I think it was, yes, in September, it was about four months later, in September, that I was pacing impatiently back and forth on the empty platform, the train platform, high-heeled light brown cowboy half-boots, tight faded blue jeans, white, no, off-white, natural-color, loose raw silk shirt with puffy sleeves to contrast with the tight blue faded denim jeans, bathed, shampooed, shaven, lemon-scented, Monsieur-Balmain-*eau de-Cologne*-ed with Monsieur-Balmain *eau de-Cologne* bought in Rouen years earlier in that beautiful yellow old-fashioned apothecary, I mean, chemist, bottle, flat vertical cheeks, a light brown leather, no, tanned orange face, a single red-rose stem in my hand like an epée, a fencer on the *piste* fencing with nothing, with space, with empty space, with her prolonged absence that just wouldn't go away, lunge, thrust, retreat, lunge, thrust, retreat, lunge, lunge, thrust, almost literally so, don't know how or why but after a while the rose stem was gone, useless, stripped of most leaves and petals, had to get a new one to welcome her with, rushed back out to get a fresh one from one of the flower ladies, old women outside the station, the plaza in front, cost a fortune, the other one gotten cheaper, at a reasonable price in town, worried would miss the train, her arrival, rushed like crazy, like always, no need, no need to worry, something was going on weather-wise where she was coming from, in the west, thunderstorms, or floods, or something, they were announcing changes in arrival time, now half an hour later, now two hours, now less, any time, now half an hour later again, at one point I think they said four hours and I nearly flipped out, it's god! it's this monster of a god who's torturing me, who's toying with me, enjoying seeing me squirm on this platform as if in a hot skillet! but then unexpectedly they said the train had come, HAD come! and there improbably appeared the huge silent head of the engine, the diesel engine, coming slowly from around the curve of the bend, as if afraid it'd do something to itself if it moved faster and in the end wouldn't make it after all, looking like a giant, super giant, super, super giant fish with a prognathous jaw, not a whale, a fish, and not a shark either with its receding chin, like that super ugly fish with the jaw that sticks way out whose name I can't remember, except much, much, much, much bigger, thousands, many thousands times bigger, and kept advancing, the engine, the train kept advancing slowly, getting nearer and nearer, and I saw an open window, a black open window in one of the cars with a white hand, a white batiste handkerchief hand sticking out of it and waving, and then a pair of huge pearl-gray eyes looking in my direction, and she was there! we charged up the stairs to the terminal, the station, two at a time, holding hands, no, slow down, one at a time, slowly, holding, I in my left hand, she in her right one, the two respective, that is respectively right and left handles, loops of the big, heavy soft clothes bag she brought along, I with her smaller suitcase in my right one in addition, then clambered up the walls of the shaft to the apartment together with the old clanky elevator, our collective fingernails scratching determinedly on the masonry surface, the next morning, no, not the next one, the following, no, wrong again, the one after that, the third one, the third morning, when the time had come, when there was a reason, I took a picture of her, she in a loose white, no, cream silk shirt, sitting at the round dining table, the hair pulled back, the bun in the back not showing, a strand or two strayed off, imparting spontaneity, naturalness to the image, the lips, the thinner upper one and the fuller lower shiny and red, as if with lipstick although without it, gently touching, gently tending toward a smile, the gently rounded chin below dimpled in the middle as if with a gentle push, a peck of a finger, the two huge pearl-gray eyes even huger, softly shining, softly staring into the camera, into my greedy single Cyclops eye, still have it, still have the picture somewhere, no, not somewhere, on the table, always on the table, on the

Yuriy Tarnawsky

writing table in my study, in my room, in my writhing writing room, on my writhing writing table right now, sometimes unexpectedly, she'd push me into the armchair, say, Sit! and start dancing, silently, without music, just to the sound of her breathing, the soft sibilant sexy sound of her sexy breathing, air coming in and escaping through her nostrils, between her lips, parts of her body like items of clothing, dark items of clothing stretched out of shape in their flight through the air, hastily tossed now this way, now that, with haste, impatience, unable to hold back the urge to quench, satisfy the passion, urge, I was left speechless, amazed, stared with my mouth open, god, is this true? for real? is this happening with me? for me? to me? what luck! how lucky I am! I never expected it, never dreamed of it, never knew such things existed, such a person existed, what luck! in the afternoons we'd go exploring the park, the woods along the slope, the winding, tricky paths to the huge river below, to the big water when one day, I mean, one night she'd stand in, both of us would stand in, on a moonlit spring, no, moonlit early summer night, waiting for a white balloon to free itself from under her shirt, from under her chin, her gently curving, gently pecked, dimpled chin and float, its string wiggling like the tail of a determined, stubborn, vigorous spermatozoa toward the full white moon way up in the sky, in the zenith, in a flock of others, the day she was leaving, a month or so later, middle of October, in early afternoon, I was lying in bed stretched out on my back, resting, prolonging what I'd just lived through, not wanting to let go of it, she having already washed up, had just started to get dressed, still fully naked, stood with her back turned to the window, to the glass door leading onto the balcony in the back, overlooking the courtyard, was partly turned toward me, her nearly flat, barely convex young girl's abdomen casting a vaguely lilac shadow on her pubis, and I heard the janitor, the superintendent caretaker that looked like an underpensioned retired professor with his gold-rimmed glasses, spectacles, who was doing something there, sweeping, or picking things up, or fixing something, call out to his Down Syndrome son, No, Sebastian, no! and she said, Oscar's a nice name. Should we call him that? and I said, I was thinking of Sebastian. I really like it. What do you think? and she said, Sebastian's nice too. I like it. Sure.

9

SHE DID COME, I mean, I did come, that is, I did go back there many years later, very many, fifty at least, more, more than fifty, it doesn't matter how many, the number being so high, it doesn't matter exactly how many, came back both in life and in a dream, dream more vivid, remember it better, headed straight for the cemetery, which lies on that side of town, so you come to it first, it would have been strange to go into town before visiting the cemetery, anyway, headed there first, you turn right up a little narrow road, the first one past the first few houses, right, up, up, left, up, straight, and there it is, the cemetery, the cemetery's on the left side, I leave the car on the left too, facing uphill, it's closer, near the gate, get out, go inside, the spot is maybe twenty paces on the left, I think, strange, but I think I remember, I look there and there, exactly there it is, the headstone rising up above the tall thick grass, her name clearly spelled, chiseled out on it, as if possessed, I throw myself down on my knees and start pulling it up, pulling up the grass, pulling it up by the roots, fistfuls of it, throwing it away, behind me, to the sides, next to other graves, upon them, as if possessed, desperate, as if my life, someone's life, as if her life depended on it, as if it'd save her, bring her back to life, as if its roots had dug themselves into my throat like fingers and were choking me to death, grab, pull, throw, grab, pull, pull, throw, grab, grab, pull, pull, pull, throw, the grave becoming cleaner, cleaner and cleaner, the hard white stone shining through, eventually all clear, clean, like a freshly washed fresh face, white, without blemishes, the grave's face, not her face, but still clear and fresh, and then a noise, a sound, attracts, grabs my attention, loud, high-pitched, unbroken, rising and falling, wailing, like a female voice wailing, coming from behind my left, a little behind, the grave's clean, so it's alright, I stand up on my knees, turn, and look, it's her, it's she standing on the side of a freshly-dug grave, playing a violin, facing the grave, on its very edge, weaving this way and that as violin players do while performing, playing, it looks like she's just gotten out of bed because she's barefoot and is wearing a night shirt that reaches just below her knees, her legs and arms are thin, with bones showing under the loose skin, ribs stand out on her chest where it's visible under her chin, and her thin, sinewy neck protrudes above it, her long lanky hair falls in two curving lines around her face like the musical f sign but without the dash, one the right way, the other one reversed, it's red, the hair is red, not hair-red but bright red like certain shades of nail polish or lipstick, I'm surprised but then I notice it's fall, the leaves on the trees have turned, are yellow and red, red close to the color of her hair, so it's right that her hair is this color, I'm satisfied, remember the opening lines of Verlaine's poem *"Les sanglots longs des violons de l'automne blessent mon coeur d'une langueur monotone,"* I'm calmed even more, wonder why she's playing the violin, she didn't play the violin before except the piano, sweetly, softly, I'd listen sometimes to her playing, when I was little, sitting on the floor leaning against the wall next to the room she was in, my eyes shut, almost falling asleep, but then tell myself, she's no longer here, it's different over there, that's why, I'm satisfied again, notice there's a mound of earth piled up high on the other side of the grave, yellow, mustard-colored like a bush with its leaves that have changed color in the fall, a little group of people stand before it, between it and the grave, as if sheltering under it as if under a bush, about a dozen or so, huddling together as if from wind or cold, or danger, fear, even better, adults all except for two children up front, a boy and a girl,

65

the boy about ten, the girl a few years older, the boy stands closer to the edge of the grave than the girl, too close, dangerous, he might fall in, I worry but then think of the line in the poem, *"Pareil à la feiulle morte,"* for some strange reason am calmed down by it again, feel the boy will be alright, am curious now about the grave, what it's like inside? I walk up to it, look, it's deep, many feet deep, more like a well than a grave, there's some water on the bottom, it glitters, reflecting the sky, the coffin's there, it's tiny, the size of a shoe box rather than a coffin, it's shaped like a shoe box too, not like a coffin, how's she going to fit into it? it's a different world from ours, I tell myself again, don't worry about it, it'll be fine, I look up and see her playing as before, oblivious of everything, weaving this way and that, producing the shrill, endless, wailing sound, think again of the phrase *"Pareil à la feiulle morte,"* then suddenly I'm at my grandmother's house, it's gone, there's a huge pile of debris in place of it, a couple of stories high, higher than the house used to be, bricks, wooden beams, roof shingles, fragments of white walls, door- and window frames, shards of glass, contents that were there before, broken-up furniture, bedlinen, clothing, kitchen utensils, a mess, an ungodly mess, it doesn't bother me however, as if I'd expected it, as if I'd seen it already, the field beyond the house, beyond the pile of debris, is all clear however, same as it used to be, our house, the house that father and mother built and in which we hadn't lived even for a moment, stands at the end of it, on the slope that rises there, along the road that runs along it, it looks different than what I remember it looked like, not a modern villa with big windows and balconies, built of bricks and stucco, but square and squat, with many small windows, and built of gray stone, looking more like a dungeon, a prison, than a private home, although like our home, it's still three stories high, curious, I walk to it, cross the field, go around to the front door, and try to open it, pressing down on the door handle, immediately the whole house explodes with loud dog barking, I look up and see heads of dogs sticking out of all the windows, huge vicious dogs, two or three in each window, mostly black, it seems, eyes ablaze, bulging, popping out, teeth bared, big and white, sharp, lips curled back, the clipped triangular ears leaning forward, trying to help out, help the teeth, a racket, an ungodly racket, like hundreds of metal cans or pots being hit repeatedly with something heavy and hard, not a spoon, but a metal rod or something, you'd expect it perhaps from the side of the house I'm at but it's coming from everywhere, from the sides too, from the two other sides, and I'm sure it's the same on the opposite side, the one facing my grandmother's house, it's frightening, it's a dog prison or something, a dog house, there's no room for me here, I'd better get away, I step back, turn around, walk down the road downhill, toward the town, our house was all alone but soon I'm in among other houses, buildings, but they're not buildings except heaps of rubble, like grandmother's house, they're tall, taller than normal one-story or even two-story houses are, I walk on, the same's all around me, except no, not the same, the heaps are not of rubble but of broken chairs, hundreds upon hundreds of them, former building after building now a giant heap of broken wooden chairs with straight backs, strange, where did they all come from? I walk on, the same everywhere, mountain upon mountain of broken wooden chairs, the town is different than I remember, bigger, with many streets, I get lost in them, trudge on and on, grow tired, god, when will this end? when will I get out into the open? be free? but I see no open space, so I trudge on and on, grow more and more tired, my strength's abandoning me, I must rest, must sit down, but where? I need a table, I can probably pull a halfway decent chair out of one of the piles around me but I need a table to place it at, how can you sit in a chair, resting if there isn't a table next to it? why isn't there one, just one, just one miserable old table will do, it's unfair, I start crying, tears run down my face, I can barely see where I'm going, eventually somehow I'm out of the labyrinth and am lying on my back on the ground, there's grass growing before my eyes, blocking my view, seems to be sprouting right out of my neck, throat, I must be back in the cemetery, it seems, and am overgrown with grass as my mother's grave was earlier, it's terrible, it'll kill me eventually, choke me to death, it is already, it is already choking me, I find it hard to breathe, I try to struggle, to pull the grass by the roots out of my throat, it's hard to do, the grass resists as if alive, it chokes me harder and harder, the more I try to free myself from it, the more it chokes me, I struggle with it as if with a person, try to roll over, sit up, but now it's not grass I'm fighting with but fingers, long woman's fingers, I'm outraged, desperate, why? why is this being done to me? who's doing it? what could I have done to some woman so that she'd want to choke me to death? it's my mother, I suddenly realize, it's my mother's long fingers I just saw playing the violin! it's her! but why? why would my mother want to kill me?" I'm her son! Mother, mother! I scream, It's me, your son! Why are you trying to kill me? I'm your son! I'm your son! but she continues unswayed, as if not hearing me, squeezing my neck harder and harder, digging her fingernails deeper and deeper into my flesh, I feel myself blacking out, soon I will, I mobilize all my force, scream as hard as I can, Nooooo!, free myself from her clutch, and wake up, it is only after I caught my breath and calmed down, I realized what had been happening, It was because she didn't want you to be alone, I told myself.

10

WHY DO I keep looking at the door all the time as if expecting to see someone there? who? my wife? my wife back home from work? no, it's not the time yet, I'm sure, and besides, it's not a woman, a female figure I hope to see, but a man, I'm sure of that, the feeling I'd have if it were a woman would be different, I'd be able to tell it, I know, it's someone very close to me, a man, very, very close, as close as it could be, like I myself, for instance, I? myself? who's come to see me, to check up on me, to chase away my loneliness? crazy! how can you visit yourself to check up on you and chase your loneliness away? it's not that of course but something similar, very, very similar, very, very close, my father? my father? I've just been to his funeral, right? so how could I be expecting him to come to see me? crazy! no, not crazy, I'm not sure I've just been to a funeral, in fact, I'm sure I haven't been to a funeral just now, perhaps recently, meaning within the last few weeks or months, but even that is doubtful, sometime, yes, I've been to funerals, to many of them in fact, but recently, it's doubtful, although not impossible, but if so, if yes, if I've been recently to a funeral , then why would it have had to be his? why of necessity his? it could have been someone else who'd died, a man perhaps, but not my father, but even if it were my father who'd died, recently or otherwise, I could still expect, still want to see him standing in the doorway, having come to see me, to chase away my loneliness, in fact it's quite normal, even likely, very likely, very, very likely, with any person, any person you loved who's passed away, you're likely to love him/her even more than before, even more than before he/she died, because you miss him/her more, miss him/her precisely because he/she has died, is gone, because you know he/she won't ever come to see you, because you know you'll never see him/her again, so even if my father's gone, if he has died, I may more than ever want to see him standing in the doorway, having come to see me to chase away my loneliness like he did that one time in that bleak godforsaken town I moved to when I got my first job, my first full-time professional job after graduating from college, after getting my diploma, and lived in that bleak rented room in the horrible-looking bleak brick house on the bleak street with similar bleak brick houses on it standing shoulder to shoulder as far as the eye can see in both directions, and one Sunday, Sunday afternoon I think it was, yes, Sunday afternoon it was for sure because he had to be back home that night, he was coming up by train and I was supposed to meet him at the station down below by the river, and feeling down, feeling tired, tired more psychologically than physically, lay down on top of the bed fully dressed to wait for the right time to get up and go to welcome him, a short walk to the station, not much more than or perhaps not even a mile away, and fell asleep, I fell asleep, a painful dreamless sleep like a square wooden peg driven deep into my flesh, brain, and suddenly woke up feeling there was someone in the doorway, and as I opened my eyes, saw him standing there, with the door still open behind him, the smile on his always tightly closed lips and the gleam in his gray eyes silver, shiny like the gray hair on his temples, I shot up instantly awake, awake but with the painful square wooden peg of the sleep still in my flesh, brain, ran up to him, threw my arms around his shoulders, felt the hard bones hot under his short-sleeved shirt, he carried his jacket draped over his arm in the common European custom, it was a hot day, summers were devilishly hot in that godforsaken place, the room still relatively cool in the brick house though, it was early afternoon, probably not much more than an hour past twelve, around one PM, I kissed him on the cheeks, apologized, explained, it's nothing, he said, except he was worried about me, something may have happened, a heart attack, a stroke, living alone, young, but you never know, luckily he had my address with him, got a taxi, and came, the door was unlocked, I'd left it unlocked, he couldn't call because I didn't have a phone, it was supposed to be a temporary stay, which luckily it was, I ushered him in, closed the door, tried to be hospitable, make him comfortable, pulled the chair away from the table, made him sit in it, I on the bed, on the edge of the squeaky iron bed, he was thirsty, did I have anything cold to drink? no, but I got him some water, some lukewarm water out of the tap over the washbasin stuck to the wall in the corner, he drank, but I felt guilty, Let's go out, I said, There's a soda fountain place nearby on Main Street, how far was it? he asked, he couldn't stay very long, What? I said, You've just come, having traveled all that distance and you want to go back already? the hair on my head nearly stood on end, although it wasn't out of character for him, it was to be expected, I shouldn't have been surprised, he pulled out the train schedule out of one of his coat pockets, there was a train back in a little under three hours, he had to take it, he had to be back home that night, his job, and there was an insurance premium bill for the car arriving next day, he had to make sure he'd pay it on time, But dad! But father! it didn't help, he could never be persuaded, swayed, would never permit his mind to be changed, alright, we had more than two hours, we went out, went to the soda fountain place, a Norman Rockwell joint, near empty at the time, with an old man and a cop at the counter, the cop not in tall boots, those high leather gaiters or whatever you call them as in the Norman Rockwell picture, cover, and no kid on a stool next to him with a little bundle of something wrapped in a red kerchief on the floor, sat down ourselves at the counter, on the tall uncomfortable red-toped chrome stools that always threaten to impale you, he had a ginger ale, a cold one, then another one, I, a club soda, cold too of course, we walked down the empty streets to the station, to the river afterwards, past the dusty black show windows of the closed-down stores, closed-down abandoned warehouses, factories, breweries, vacant lots with a chipped leftover piece of brick here and there left over from torn-down buildings after the debris had been removed, I speaking to him with images of the loneliness I carried in me rather than words, there was a restaurant by the river, an Italian place, with a big boat with a canopy over it tethered to the shore as part of it, used as a dining room, one of its three or four big dining rooms, it being a two minutes' walk from the station, we sat there, at a table on the river side of the boat, the floor under us gently heaving, moving up and down like the chest of a man breathing evenly in his sleep, moving up and down with the tide, as it, the tide, the tide of the ocean some eighty miles away ebbed or flowed, the sunlight reflected off the water found its way between the dense creeper on the trellis on my right into my eyes, forcing me to fidget on the chair so as not to be bothered by it, it playing silly little games of hide and seek on his face across the table from me but without apparently interfering with his seeing because he didn't move around like me and didn't complain, had broiled fish, some flaky tasty white fish, red snapper probably served with a green sauce, delicious, delicious to me, although he barely nibbled on it, making sure to keep his looks of a skeleton, not on purpose, of course, but still, with the same effect, cold beer to drink, quaffed down eagerly by both of us, then, with forty-five minutes to go he became restless, started fidgeting, there was no way he could miss the train, no way, but we're two minutes away, we'll get there on time for sure, no, it may arrive early and then he'll miss it, half an hour to go, thirty-five minutes actually, I think, I gave in, having gulped down what I could manage of the fish, I paid up, we left, and waited forty-five minutes for the train to come, it was late, he had put his jacket on but under it his bones still felt hard and hot as I embraced and kissed him on the cheeks as he was boarding the train, I planned to read to him that play I'd been working on since moving to that town, almost exclusively on Sundays, I mean, working on the play almost exclusively on Sundays, late Sunday afternoons, in a restaurant at the station in the city over a cup of tea, about an hour or two each time, waiting for the train to take me back home, back to my room from having stayed with him, at his place, which happened almost every weekend, by train, because I didn't have a car yet at the time, that happened later that fall, that is, I planned to read to him what I'd done so far of the play, which was probably about half of it, some twenty pages or so, but didn't, not only because there was no time for it but also because as soon as I saw him in the doorway I realized it wasn't the proper time or place to do it, a lonely son reading a play about loneliness to a lonely father in a lonely place, that is I wouldn't have read it to him even if there'd been time to do it, *The Gnashing of Teeth* it, the play, was called, referring to "the weeping and

77

gnashing of teeth in the impenetrable outer darkness" we're threatened to be thrown into if we don't behave as we are told by the all-mighty, the all-cruel father of us all, it was based on Kierkegaard's *Fear and Trembling* and *Sickness unto Death*, on the former mostly, fear and trembling the joy of being happy with love would go stale, grow moldy from the repetition of the daily routine of being together, so it being a defense of solitude, of loneliness, in it I first had him, Kierkegaard, and his betrothed, the woman he loved but refused to marry, what's her name, Karen? Karina? Karina Molson? no, not Molson, Molson's a brand of beer, Canadian beer, Olson? Karina Olson? no, Olsen, Regina Olsen, yes, that's it, Regina Olsen, she married eventually her tutor but never stopped loving him, Kierkegaard, poor woman, she and her husband would read his, Kierkegaard's works before going to bed, I mean in bed before falling asleep, before turning out the light, blowing out the candle, before her being mounted, although I don't know how much mounting went on in that marriage, I suspect not much, Denmark's a flat country, the closest thing to mountains in it I know of is the Belgian town of Bergen where that big auto rally, the auto races take place each year, anyway, planned her and him to have a verbal, rhetorical fencing match on a black velvet *piste,* she for yes, for staying together, he for no, for being apart, on a stage hung on all sides with black velvet, the two dressed all in black with white lace collars, she, that of a fine young Scandinavian lady, he, of a Scandinavian Lutheran pastor, but decided against it, that is, changed it to both of them in nightshirts, sitting on chamber pots in a bedroom with flowery Scandinavian wallpaper on the walls, this after I saw that play called *Three Urns,* no, *Urns,* just *Urns,* I think, yes, *Urns* by that famous, popular playwright Samuel Adams? Sam Adams? no, Sam Adams is a brand of beer, a New England, Boston, I think, beer, I don't know what's wrong with me that I have beer on my mind all the time today, Sam Buckett? Samuel Buckett? no again, Samuel Beckett, he's called, yes, Samuel Beckett, they used garbage cans, three corrugated iron garbage cans in that production, so I thought, chamber pots, two big old-fashioned flowered ceramic Scandinavian chamber pots would be good for them to have it out in the open, in public, well, not out in the open, actually under night shirts, but still in public, anyway, she for yes, for being together, he for no, for staying apart, Graveyard, graveyard is what Kierkegaard means in Danish, churchyard literally, *kierk* meaning church, its cognate, and *gaard* meaning yard, a cognate of English yard and garden, doublets, these are called, an interesting linguistic phenomenon, words in a language having the same origin, ancestor, but sounding different and having sometimes a different meaning, in English for instance we have church and kirk, a Scots English word meaning the same, and shirt and skirt, both of the second in the two pairs having come in through the Norse invaders, anyway again, Graveyard, what could you expect from a man named Graveyard other than arguing for solitude, the eternal solitude of lying in the grave? I can hear some stirrings, some noise downstairs, noise coming from downstairs, it couldn't be my father, of course, he's gone, long gone, or maybe recently gone, it doesn't matter, still gone, gone for good, forever, he was old when I saw him then and I was young, so he would be *uralt*, super old now, he's gone, gone for sure, it's my son I'm waiting for, not him, of course, my son Sebastian, I remember now, he went out to get something for himself or me, medicine or a drink, an electrolyte drink for me, for instance, and maybe for himself too, I think he exercises a lot like I used to, and is back now, Sebastian! Sebastian! is that you? can you hear me? he can't hear me, my voice is too weak, I can barely hear it myself, Sebastian!

11

MOTHER CARRIED THE child in a white moon and we walked through the dense darkness under the tall leafy trees, the moon still not up in the sky, either not out from behind the horizon or hiding somewhere low, certainly not behind clouds because you could see stars here and there in the tears in their tattered shapes, the flaming torches we carried high in our hands not doing much to dispel, dilute the darkness, spewing more smoke than casting light with their dirty tar-smelling flames, the candles, the four candles in the wreath on her head not helping out at all, barely casting light on her face, making it look strange at times, changed, not like herself, as if the ritual, in which we were going to take part had taken effect already, had turned her into what she was going, was supposed to be, but staying lit, the candles staying lit, even if at times threatening to go out, our bare feet, or at least mine, contributing more than our eyes to our progress, making out on their own the direction of the smooth, slightly slippery clay path moist with dew or something, the sharp stones or an occasional twig upon it hurting their pampered, city-slicker soles, it, the path meandering along uncertainly, unsteadily, going now right, now left but in the end always forward, forward and down, down to the left, toward the huge river, the vast body of water it seemed to sense there, as we unconsciously did with some mysterious organ deep inside our bodies, both of us, that is, she and I, barefoot as I said, she with a wreath of flowers and four candles in it on her head and in a loose long-sleeved shirt of coarse homespun linen reaching to the middle of her calves, I, in a long-sleeved shirt open at the neck and matching pants with tight, somewhat short tight legs, the torches, candles, wreaths, and clothes, all, provided by the organizers, we descending more and more with time and with the distance traveled on the path, our eyes eventually espying, discerning here and there before us, higher up or down below, specks of fire, flickering light, they eventually turning into trickles, then streams, raging brooks of fire, flames, flames of the torches, crowds of the specs of light, of the light of the candles, all eventually collecting in a sizeable crowd, a group of people, fifty, a hundred, perhaps two hundred, couples all, the two of us among them, the torches were collected, held by minders, the women took off their wreaths, being careful with the candles, making sure they stayed in, stayed lit, put them, put the wreaths, in the hands of their partners, still being careful with the candles, clothes were taken off, clothes of both men and women, wreaths changed hands, once, twice, in the end winding up back in the women's hands, their candles still lit, candles still carefully guarded, clothes were put in separate piles, separate neat piles, the latter marked, remembered, the women waded into the river holding their wreaths carefully in their hands, minding the candles, making sure they stayed lit, waded up to the waist in water, higher, set them, set the wreaths on the water, still careful, still making sure the candles stayed lit, propelled them, propelled the wreaths, made them float, immersed themselves up to their chins, some higher, all the way, all the way to submergence, all, everyone giggled, laughed, ran out onto the bank, we, men, ran along it, the bank, keeping our eyes on our partner's wreath, then waded into the river on command, dove in, swam, each eager, determined to catch his partner's wreath, otherwise a problem, otherwise no good, serious potential trouble, I desperate, never took my eye off her wreath, didn't dive head in, always kept my eye on it, her wreath, got out of breath, caught it, the wreath, hurray! it'll be good, it'll work!

some didn't, didn't catch their partner's wreath, somebody else's, laughed, made a joke out of it, I got a better deal! but it was clear they worried, worried deep down, I got out, there she was, I showed it, the wreath to her, placed it on her head, the candles still lit, she already knew, she hugged me, we hugged, kissed, it's great! it worked! It'll work! hugged more, firmer, kissed longer, hotter, we found our pile, our pile of clothes, rubbed ourselves dry with our hands, alone and each other, rubbed ourselves dry as best we could, it wasn't bad, surprising, still cold though, both cold, shivered, teeth chattered, pulled our clothes on, the wreath still on her head, but the candles gone somewhere, don't remember, she, the shirt, pulled on the shirt, I, the pants and the shirt, rubbed ourselves dry with them, with our hands through them, alone again and each other, rubbed ourselves dry pretty well, surprisingly well, the clothes not wet, not wet at all, well, a little, wet a little, barely noticeable, damp, essentially damp as if from sweating, we feeling warm now, quite warm, the fabric, the coarse homespun linen undoubtedly, thick, absorbing, not like the thin, horrible synthetic crap we're forced to wear nowadays, then, later, away from the river somehow, high up on the tall bank, in the clearing in a wood, tall trees all around like dark giant men, the torches gone,

gone again somewhere, a big bonfire, that is, a bunch of big bonfires, maybe a dozen or so, no, not a dozen, half a dozen maybe, five or six bonfires, with a dozen or so couples around each, so about one hundred people or so taking part, yes, that's right, about fifty coupes or one hundred people, men and women in circles, in two circles around the bonfire, women on the inside, closer together, men on the outside, farther apart, women smaller, white, men taller, dark, younger, kid brothers of the big older brother trees behind them, all holding hands, moving now in the same direction, now in the other one, the men and women circles moving now in the same direction, now in the other, in the opposite one, everyone singing songs, weird, wonderful songs, something about couples, couples being one, the phrase, One couple, repeated over and over, something like One couple, not quite the same but close, very, very close, One couple, one couple, one couple, repeated over and over, meaning obviously the couple should stay one, together, then the word, marriage, a word like marriage, not quite marriage but very close, very, very close to marriage, and, topple, the word topple, very close to topple, the phrase, obviously that the marriage shouldn't topple, or fall apart, Marriage topple, marriage topple, marriage topple, repeated over and over, and then the end, the magnificent fiery finale of couples jumping over fire, over bonfires, while holding hands, each couple jumping together over their bonfire, man on the right, woman on the left, he holding her right hand in his left and the wreath in his right, she raising the hem of her shirt with her left, he tossing the wreath into the flames while going over them, a symbolic taking of her virginity, I presume, both giving out a wild scream, she of pain and joy, he just of joy, the day she was leaving, beginning of October, I think it was, yes, middle of October, in early afternoon, but not that year, a year earlier, when I did that pacing on the train platform, I was lying in bed stretched out on my back, resting, prolonging what I'd just lived through, not wanting to let go of it, she having already washed up, had just started to get dressed, still fully naked, stood with her back turned to the window, to the glass door leading onto the balcony in the back, overlooking the courtyard, was partly turned toward me, her nearly flat, barely convex young girl's abdomen casting a vaguely lilac shadow on her pubis, and I heard the janitor, the superintendent caretaker that looked like an underpensioned retired professor with his gold-rimmed glasses, spectacles, who was doing something there, sweeping, or picking things up, or fixing something, call out

to his Down Syndrome son, No, Oscar, no! and she said,
Oscar's a nice name. Should we call him that? and I said, I
was thinking of Sebastian. I really like it. What do you think?
and she said, Sebastian's nice too. I like it. Sure.

12

FOURTEEN DAYS OF Bach, on the organ, in a church, St. Thomas, was it? don't remember, probably not, St. Thomas was in Leipzig, where his remains were eventually moved to in 1949, so this was probably something else, St. Luke or St. Mathew, something like that, but St. Thomas too, it's possible, last week of May and the first of June, I think, late afternoon or early evening, no, must have been early evening, couldn't have been afternoon weekdays, people working, wrong atmosphere, weekends yes, weekdays no, the performer, organist, what's his name? someone big and powerful, Powell? Big Powell? no, can't remember, doesn't matter, good, very good, at the time perhaps the best in the world, so early evening, still light outside, daytime, the air greenish golden like Portuguese wine, vinho verde, we waited outside, on the sidewalk for a while, a huge crowd at the gate of paradise, heaven, then they let us in one by one, in a file, felt good, restriction mirroring that of what was coming, what we were going to hear, strictness, control, feeling, emotions controlled, that is governed, watched over like children guided by concerning, capable parents, a real good feeling, being looked after, braced, the hard wooden pews feeling good too, matching what was coming, what we were going to hear, what we knew was coming, what we knew we were going to hear, strictness, control, guidance, great anticipation, hushed non-stillness, people whispering in the stillness, knowing, hoping, it would soon end, end any instant, this instant, and then it did, the sound like a giant bird's, music eagle's wing, single wing moving the still air and you knew the anticipated moment, the world-changing, game-changing change had taken place, thunders had descended from the sky and made their home in the space, the great nave of the church, everyone watching them through the sound in their ears as if through imagers in their eyes, that is in their minds, thunder, the sounds of thunder being drilled in the bootcamp of music, the drill sergeant the organist Big Powell, Big E. Powell, that's right, Big E. Powell, I remember now, so, the drill sergeant the organist Big E. Powell, not Bach, Bach, the major, colonel, general in charge of the boot camp, the defense minister, commander in chief of the army, the army of music, theoretician who came up with the rules of the drill, created, defined them, made soldiers out of sounds you hear all day at home, in the woods, in the street around you, the one who made a great army, a disciplined Prussian army out of the chaos of noise, this going on for two hours, and then thirteen days more two hours each time, so fourteen times two, meaning twenty-eight hours total, or there about, more most likely in reality, some days it may have been more than two hours, maybe two and a half, but never less, pretty sure of that, would have noticed, felt cheated, but didn't, so it may have been thirty hours or more, something like that, Toccata and Fugue in D-Minor, of course, but that's a tiny little peak sticking up on the huge unmelting tip of the iceberg among other peaks, many of them on the peak, and then the rest of it, the rest of the giant iceberg below, nine times more, toccatas and fugues, preludes and fugues, fugues alone, passacaglias, fantasias, some of them with toccatas, others alone, sonatas, concertos, pedal exercises, chorales, more, the knowledge, awareness growing, opening up like eyes in amazement, opening wide until they were, the mind was ready to pop, a thorough, complete revision of the vision of the world, life, man, wow! so this is what man is capable of achieving, of creating such incredible beauty! and such incredible beauty can and does exist and I am capable of creating it! wow! wow! wow! I have to change my life, be careful from now on how I live, can't waste a second on something unnecessary, trivial, must devote every single milli-, micro-, terasecond of it to trying to achieve it, to get as close as possible to reaching that goal, to creating such incredible beauty, to get as far as I am capable of going, it changed my life, I was never the same again and never strayed away for an instant from that goal to this very moment of my life, when I came home that first night, no, not night, late afternoon or early evening, it was still light, the air still golden-green like vinho verde, so it must have been Sunday, the first day Sunday and the last Saturday, yes, the concert must have started then at maybe two in the afternoon, soon after the mass and would have been over by about four-thirty, then an hour to hour and a half for the trip home, so it would have been about six PM when I got home, and when I got home that late afternoon/early evening, the apartment, space looked different, don't know how to describe it, but different, the same line between the wall and the ceiling but something about it different, perhaps not the line itself, its image, but its meaning, relation to the world, the same about the ceiling and the wall themselves, the other ceilings and walls in the apartment, the rooms, the furniture in them, the windows, the world outside them, me, I myself, different, firmer somehow, more there, even more important perhaps, I more important for sure, independent, sovereign, strong, one among equals, among other independent, sovereign, strong entities, objects, beings in the world, a great feeling, what a great feeling! beauty all around, having witnessed Bach's beauty making the world beautiful too for some reason, the sun, already low, was shining in through the windows, its rays tinged green by the tall evergreens, rhododendrons, arborvitaes, yews, whatever those plants were that were filling out the courtyard of the garden apartment building complex, golden green sunshine, my chest bursting, exploding with joy at seeing it, the world, witnessing its magnificence around me, being a magnificent part of it myself, opened a bottle of vinho verde I had in the refrigerator and drank it, merging with everything around me and beyond into one inseparable whole, golden green light and liquid, and the same for the next thirteen days, not exactly the same, of course, you never step into the same river twice, but essentially the same, the same in its essence, I don't think vinho verde every night after that, for instance, yes, yes, of course! three weeks later I moved into that first house I bought a few weeks earlier, having to wait for the closing, brought out that little round table of red cherry wood with its folding wings, set it in the corner between the main house and the bathroom sticking out from it in the back that was added on later to have a bathroom handy on the main floor since there wasn't one there before, set a chair by it, sat in it, opened a bottle of the Portuguese semi-effervescent wine, Lancers, I think it was called, yes, Lancers, and drank it, drank it all, roaming leisurely with my eyes through the garden which was now mine, my mouth filled with the bubbly fruity liquid, trying to force its way out in red and white globules through the corners of my smiling mouth, Sebastian! Sebastian! Sebastian! of course! Bach was called in daily life Sebastian and not Johann or Johann Sebastian, Johann was sort of a prefix, label, denoting a man belonging to the Bach family, there were Johann Something Bachs in the family through many generations, his father was called Johann Ambrosius, his older brother was named Johann Christian and his other brothers, Johann Jakob and Johann Christoph, he named two of his sons, Johann Christian and Johann Christoph, clearly after his brothers, and Johann was often used in Germany as sort of a silent pre-name, one of his godfathers for instance was Johann Georg Koch, and in his birth record it says his name is Joh.

Sebastian, so, of course, he was called Sebastian, Sebastian this and Sebastian that, no, Sebastian! yes, Sebastian! Sebastian! Sebastian! Sebastian! I didn't then and don't now look like him, but he wasn't always this corpulent curmudgeon, there are prints of him looking trim and reasonably handsome, oh, those lascivious oiled eyes looking out of their corners from under the slightly puffy eyelids, the perfectly formed black, shiny eyebrows that used to drive girls crazy, wet between their legs! oh that swelling next to the corner of the archaically smiling mouth as if from a bite in a kiss of a girl gone wild with passion, from which the bubbles of the semi-effervescent rose Portuguese wine were trying to find their way out into the open!

13

THE DOOR EMPTY, still? already? again? who should be there? a man? a woman? young? old? my father, mother, wife, daughter, son? Sebastian? Sebastian! Sebastian! no reply, mother! father! no reply, will call my wife, what's her name? Ana? Ena? Ina? Ona? Una? have forgotten, something ending in an "a," Aaaa! Aaaa! Aaaa! Aaaa! no reply, no answer, the ending doesn't work, where are they all? where are they? I don't hear them, downstairs, they must be downstairs, the house is big, they're busy, quiet but busy, engrossed in something, I'm weak, my voice is weak, they don't hear me, Sebastian! Sebastian! father! mother! wife! Aaaa! Aaaa! Aaaa! nothing, no sound, no reply, but I don't think I scream, I barely whisper, I'm far away, should go to the end of the hallway and scream down the staircase, then they'll hear me, they're all there, gathered together, in a circle, having a pow-wow, a debate what to do about me, with me, they're having a meal gathered around a big round table, a table I've never seen before, I haven't been there for a while, for a long time, god knows how long, god knows what it looks like, what it's like down there, the furniture may have all been changed, old taken away, new brought in, new people, strangers may have moved in, lodgers, to help out with the expenses, I don't contribute any more, don't work, my pension has been getting more and more meager, smaller and smaller year by year, maybe has stopped coming, I may have had to do something, confirm I'm still alive and haven't done it, so I've been declared dead and my pension has stopped coming, so they have had to take in lodgers to help out with the expenses, taxes, heating, electricity, water, repairs, I have to get up and scream down the staircase to let them know I'm here, that I need them, one of them at least,   Aaaa! Sebastian! but I'm too weak to go all the way there, afraid, afraid I may fall down the staircase and end up at the landing on the bottom a pile of bones, a heap of lifeless bones, of lifeless, dusty bones, and what if no one answers my calls, if all I'll hear is the echo of my voice reverberating in the empty space like the movements of a corpse being shaken, being shaken in anger or desperation? what will I do then? it'll be even worse than now, it'll feel even worse, better not to know, better to hope, expect, no, I call again and hear nothing, myself, a faint echo of my voice like lifeless movements of a corpse being shaken in hope of bringing it back to life, it's empty there, empty of furniture and people,   probably, perhaps, I'm not sure of course, I may be wrong, probably, probably wrong, most likely all's fine down there, the old furniture's in its place, they're sitting there chatting quietly, discussing what to do with, for me, thinking I'm asleep, fine, don't know I want, need them, I can make it to the bathroom alright, it's right here, I've just been there, I think, to relieve myself, yes, I'll go there, open the window and scream their names, father! mother! Sebastian! Aaaa! and they'll hear me, someone will hear me through one of the windows downstairs, open or closed, doesn't matter much, windows don't block out that much sound, someone will hear me and come up to see what I want, will alert the others, they'll all come up, or one or more of them at least, a delegation, a team will come up to see what's going on with me, what I need, how they can help me, the whole bunch of them, five, six, whatever's the number, maybe some professionals too, nurses, doctors, psychologists, so seven? eight? nine? no, no professionals needed, no nurse, doctor or psychologist, just the kindred, loved ones, family in short, whoever's left, mother, mother? mother? did I have a mother? of course, I did, everyone does, how else would you come into the world without a mother? descend from heaven in a chariot, a luminous, golden chariot, *filius ex machina?* Christ! even Christ was made to need a mother rather than God the Father bringing him down to earth in some kind of visible or invisible device, crane or an ancient space capsule, I did of course have a mother but did I see her? I mean did I see her and understood I did, recorded it in my mind, consciousness? hmmm, no? yes, yes, I think I did but it was so long ago I barely remember, she was so small, I mean she looks so small to me now, not because she was small but because it was so long ago, and so far away, so far away in time and space, in years and miles from where I am now, a small, childlike figure on the horizon, on the horizon of time and space, almost a doll, a puppet, a hand puppet sticking up above the horizon some puppeteer is, or rather was manipulating, trying to amuse me, make me believe I had a mother who would stay with me, would help me grow up, become an adult, the bastard! why did you fool me, make me believe I had a mother when it was just a puppet, a hand puppet? you bastard! but enough of that for now, must stop, more later, father? father's big, large I mean, I mean father's real, normal. I see him well, tall, slender, muscular, wiry, with a face like mine except thinner, the nose thinner, thinner and sharper, cheeks smooth, smoothed down with age, silver, silver and gray, a silver-gray shine all around him, a three-dimensional, spherical silver-gray halo all around his memory, but he's not here, couldn't be, I just came back from his funeral, right? not sure, not sure I just came back from a funeral and if I did that it was his, it could have been for a friend or an acquaintance, or for a relative of a friend or an acquaintance, or someone else in my family, an uncle, aunt, nephew, or niece for instance, no, not an uncle, aunt, nephew, or niece, no, I don't and didn't have any of those, we were not a big or close family, loners, hermits, anchorites all like me, sad, a sad family, but funeral or not, I mean if it wasn't his funeral but someone else's, my father's not here, I'm sure of that, don't know why, for what reason, but I'm sure, a rule of some kind, perhaps connected with age, my age and his, I don't remember, it doesn't matter, a rule's a rule, and as to the funeral, it could have been for a total stranger, someone I didn't know and didn't even know his name, didn't even know if it was a man or a woman, or a child for that matter, I could have attended it for educational reasons for instance, I mean to learn what funerals are like, for future reference, that is, use, by accident or design, or

101

just for the heck of it, not having anything to do, for amusement, fun, to show myself I'm still alive and someone else is dead, something like that, whatever, or I could have simply read about it, a real vivid description that has stayed on in me so that I feel I've been to a funeral even though I haven't, that's all, my wife then, son, Sebastian? god, no! no! no! no! no! I shouldn't think thoughts like that, too close, too close for comfort, too dangerous, I think there's a saying, Don't call the wolf out of the forest, or something like that, don't remember in what language, Latin? maybe Latin, no, not Latin, the Latin saying's about your son being eaten by a wolf or something like that, what was it? *mea mater, meus pater, filius tuus lupus est?* no, that means, is, your son is, *mea mater, meus pater, tuum filium lupus edit? mandicat?* no, not *mandicat, mandicat* is more like, masticates, chews, we have, mandible in English, meaning, jaw, so *mandicat* is like, moves his jaws, it should be *edit*, from *edere,* to eat, we have, edible in English, so, *edit,* yes, it should be *edit, mea mater, meus pater, tuum filium lupus edit,* anyway, this one's different, meaning don't tempt your fate, in other words, maybe the powers that be have forgotten about this possibility and once they hear about it, are reminded of it, will decide to try it, to test it out on you, see how you react, squirm in the frying pan of your fate, and get something out of it, learn something about you, life, an experiment of sorts, they, the powers that be, they are scientists, scientists of sorts, empirical scientists, you form a hypothesis, test it out, and if the effects jive with the predictions, declare it a theory, that is the rule that may be safely employed from then on, yes, employed on their subjects, the unpowerful, they, the powerful, the powers that be, have parties high up there, invite close friends, associates, sit in a circle, drink champagne or dew and eat ambrosia, and look down between their spread knees to see what's going on below, observe, comment, discuss, and from time-to-time cheer at the grizzly spectacle unfolding before their eyes, unscientific but acceptable, that is, accepted, it happens, and that's all, who's going to do anything about it? they are the powers that be, it's a TV show of sorts, a series they, the powers that be watch in their leisure time after a hard day's work, late at night, before going to bed, she, my wife's at work, at least I think she is, she should be home later, I think it's getting dark outside, so she should be home soon, five thirty or thereabout, six or six-thirty maybe if she'll stop off at the supermarket to pick up something for dinner we don't have in the house or at the drugstore to get something for herself, some of those feminine, women's things having to do with complexion, beauty, or something for me, medicine perhaps or vitamins or an electrolyte drink, whatever, she does it as all, most, many, some wives do, but wait, what about climbing walls? someone climbing walls, a woman or a man, the woman in order to get away, that is getting away, the hell out of the unbearable, goddam marriage and the man out of despair, loneliness, solitude after she left, shivers running up his spine from the sound of his fingernails sliding on the smooth hard surface, leaving deep marks, the face streaming with blood from the grooves from having been scratched, one's face another tall wall you're trying to climb, happens all the time, often in this modern world, society, wasn't there such a climbing here or someplace close by recently? did I witness it, experienced, lived through it myself? has my wife left me and I'm dying here in bed in this huge empty house from which all furniture has been removed, dying of abandonment and hunger? and my son, our son, Sebastian? he's not here because he has never existed, was never born, because my wife couldn't conceive, because I couldn't get her pregnant, and she left, left me because of feeling guilty of not conceiving or because of being fed up with me because I couldn't get her pregnant, to find someone else, another man to marry and have children with? my god, my god, no! what am I saying? not this! not this at this point in my life, in this situation, when I am barely holding on! don't let it happen, don't let it be true! don't let it! I haven't lived through this, I swear, and haven't even witnessed it, I must have heard about it somewhere, read about it, imagined it, imagined it out of fear, it's all in my head, my mind, I swear! it's in my mind, in my mind, in my mind!

14

AND THIS TEN-YEAR old boy, he's sitting in a willow tree leaning over a stream watching its waters flow to exotic lands, India, Africa, Venice, dreams of riding in a gondola in one of its canals, passenger or gondolier taking a beautiful lady somewhere, watching from the window of a palazzo from behind a moss-green velvet curtain beautiful ladies who are possibly in love with him as he is with them being taken someplace in golden gondolas, hears a high-pitched woman's voice, a siren, that is, an air alarm siren calling his name, and he knows why, for what purpose, what reason, and he doesn't want to respond to it, acts like you do when they try waking you up in the morning and your body, all of you refuses, keeps pretending they aren't, that no one is trying to wake you up, that nothing is happening, that if they're trying to wake you up and you won't, they'll leave you alone and you'll sleep on, will keep on sleeping as long as you want to, and that the reason why they are trying to wake you up will go away, or even better, that it has never been

Yuriy Tarnawsky

there, has never existed, and that therefore you can safely go on sleeping, but the voice keeps calling him and he knows that even after it stops it will go on calling him in his mind, and that it will go on calling him there until he responds, until he does what it is urging him to do, which is to go to where he's being called from, and so he decides to stop pretending, and climbs off the tree, and drags himself where he's being called to, where they, that is it, his mother's body is waiting for him, dragging his black shadow along with him along the dusty path running along the stream like a small but unbelievably heavy rock behind him, no, not a rock because it'd be too jumpy, and not that heavy either, the dragging is not that heavy either and is soft too, soft because of not being jumpy, like the body of a dead animal for instance, a cat or a dog, no, not a cat, a cat too small, too light, a dog, a midsized dog, a midsized black dog, black because of the color of the shadow, or still better, like his own limp body, small, small because of his age but also because it is in the middle of summer and close to noon, that is a little after noon, and then dragging them, that is, himself and the body of the dog or his own, through dense semi-abandoned neighbors' orchards and over the tall fence enclosing the place he lives in and through the wide-open window of her bedroom inside it, and tiptoes, still dragging himself and his shadow although the latter is now almost invisible because of his being out of the sun but still of the same size and weight, that is still constituting the same burden, over to the side of the bed, and lifts the white sheet that has been pulled over her face, and sees it, that is the face looking as he'd expected it would look, and pulls the sheet back to its previous place, and they bury her a day later, and just after she's buried his father comes from somewhere far away and dangerous, but two days later goes away to possibly never come back, and he himself is forced to leave his home practically alone, and years later buys a house with tall white walls to climb them alone or with others, and when he stops climbing and wonders stark-naked in the middle of the night in the woods with a woman he loves next to him, she stark-naked too, clutching her huge pregnant belly, white and round like the full moon overhead in the cloudless sky as if holding it in her hands, then this means nothing? this means that no son named Oscar, I mean Sebastian will come out of her five or four or three or whatever months later? that this means no, that is, means yes, means nothing, nothing at all? then this means that it was just a dream, that is, fiction, in other words, a lie? but if so, then why, why you goddam sonofabitch, you almighty creator capable of turning darkness into light, nothing into earth and water and sky and all in six days so as to rest on the seventh, why you evil point-headed hunchbacked freak with your sour-smelling breath from the hatred inside you burning up your stomach and mind they keep locked up in the heavenly garret out of shame so that nobody sees you, why did you not let her womb bear the fruit, to come out into the world like so many trillions upon trillions of others before and in the future to be called Sebastian, to grow up into a man resembling his father to come one day like a handsome young angel and stand in his door? ugggggggggggggggggggggggggggggggggggggggg ggggggggggggggggggggggggggggggggggggggggggggggggggg ggggggggggggh! you bastard! but that's nothing, I mean that's not all, there were others involved, a thirteen-year old girl and a two-year old boy, and what about them? a thirteen-year-old girl who wouldn't have a mother to take, that is, lead her through the shaky, quaking ground of puberty and a two-year old boy who would never remember the warmth and taste of milk streaming out of his mother's breast and would never have the need, I mean reason, the opportunity to utter that most beautiful, most cherished, most comforting syllable of all, Ma, so, what about them, you sonofabitch, you evil point-headed hunchbacked freak with your sour-smelling breath, what about them? and what about the father who lost his father when he was twelve years old and mother when he was twenty, who was forced to take the train home from school every day, and got there late at night, and had to get up after three hours of sleep to take the train back in the morning, this for six days a week for four or five years? and after he married and had three children, following his call of duty he went away to fight the enemy of his people, and then his wife died and he didn't make it to her funeral, and in two days went away once again following his call of duty to possibly never come back, and then as they say worked his fingers, or was it elbows? to the bone, can't remember which, and climbed walls of the apartments he lived in, unable to buy a house for the rest of his life, what about him? you sonofabitch, you evil point-headed hunchbacked freak with your sour-smelling breath, what about him? but that's not all, that's nothing, common, happens all the time, every day, I mean happens to many, many if not all, like to those bits, parts of a girl or a woman, a whatever, a person, top of the skull down to the upper jaw, the rest of it under the sidewalk or not there, shoulders, arms, knees, whatever, sticking up sharp above the sidewalk, wrapped in rags, the eyes huge, frightening, beautiful, seeing all, understanding, accusing, why? why me? why you sonofabitch, you evil point-headed hunchbacked freak with your sour-smelling breath, why me? and to rub it in, I, tanned bronze, coin-lean, stride in a long runner's stride, Adidas wings on my feet, not two feet away past her/it, lock eyes with her/it, understand, agree, but move on and no more than a hundred feet away, no, not a hundred, fifty, some mere fifty feet away meet up with a beautiful blue-eyed girl, a girl about as beautiful as you can imagine, the Blue-Eyed Suzan, and melt with her in a kiss, a long, long kiss, ten, twenty, thirty seconds long, don't know exactly how many but very long, to make sure that those remnants, I mean those bits, parts, broken pieces of a person piled up back there on the sidewalk, that she/it can see it, can see it well, doesn't miss it, suffers every second of it, feels for a good long time what she/it will never experience, know, so that she/it will suffer more, but god, no, I don't mean god, I just mean but, but that's still nothing, still not all, should I begin rattling off the millions who died in concentration camps, gassed or of starvation, those who were starved to death in artificial famines, who sat for hours maybe days to die on stakes, who were burned at stakes, hanged and quartered, garroted, had chests cut open with obsidian knives and hearts ripped out, and, and, and, and, no time or space, no end, no, no, not a sonofabitch, not an evil point-headed hunchbacked freak with sour-smelling breath but a poor, miserable, helpless, quadriplegic of cosmic dimensions, faced with the task, desperate to the limit, pulled all his strength together and with his fingers and toes or maybe, no, likely just toes put together that handful of building blocks, strings, waves, quarks, whatever, sent them out into the void, nothing, and with the last ounce of energy, with the little toe on his left foot or his elbow, probably his elbow, set off the random number, I mean, event, random event generator to take over, rule in his place, and let everything happen that could, electrons, protons, neutrons, atoms, the ninety-eight, no, one hundred and eighteen, the one hundred eighteen elements, bright stars, black holes, constellations, nebulae, and us in the end, lies still now, never to move, tended by comets and bees.

15

HE GIGGLES AND runs as fast as he can on his stiff little legs, bare-footed and stark naked, down the long dark hallway toward the light at the end coming in through the door on the left, I chase after him, no, no, that's not it, it's I who's running with him on my back, I mean shoulders, he's partly dressed, undershorts and shirt, a tee-shirt, feet bare, legs down my chest while I hold onto them around the ankles, each in my hand, fast, jump up and down as I run, don't gallop, trot like a horse, to make sure he doesn't fall off, his body goes up and down on my shoulders and neck but just barely, I hold onto his ankles even harder to make sure he doesn't fall off, he likes it, giggles, we're going in the woods, we are in the woods, see those trees, big ones, yes? yes, and those rocks, big rocks? yes? yes, really big ones, yes? yes, you can't go up them, too steep, horses don't climb rocks, must follow the path, first left, then right, then left again, careful not to run into a tree, stumble and fall, oops, a wall, careful, very dangerous, for the horse, daddy, and Sebastian, it's straight and even now, can gallop a little, hop-pa, hop-pa, hop-pa, nice, huh? yes, must trot now, the path winds, be careful not to run into that big tree up ahead, the wall, not to stumble on that rock on the path, the stone, see? yes, a big one, jump over it, it was fun, right? yes, Sebastian's going hunting, hunting in the dark woods, hunting bears and rabbits, it's dangerous there, big bears, no, not true, in these woods bears are not dangerous, they're gentle, small and cuddly, teddy bears, like the one Sebastian has, Koko, he'll get another one, Sebastian will get another teddy bear, a friend for Koko, a brother, Moko, and maybe another one? Loko? or a couple-three more? Noko, Oko, and Poko? no, that'd be too many, and, besides, Oko doesn't fit into the scheme, but even two would be too many, and Loko isn't a good name, it's too nasty, so, Moko, Sebastian will get just one brother for Koko, Moko, that's all, still you have to catch them, him, teddy bears are scared of being caught, like to play games, hide and seek, hop-pa, hop-pa, hop-pa, it's the rabbits who are fierce here, big wild rabbits, the size of bears, real bears, bigger, twice as big as bears, big rabbits, with huge curved teeth sticking out up front, looking like sabers, like big long curved swords, that's why they're called saber rabbits, and also other with teeth like a pair of scissors, huge scissors, scissor rabbits they're called, you've got to be careful with them for if they attack you they'll cut off your hair, the men you see in the street with no hair, they've been attacked by those rabbits, daddy? no, daddy's not been caught, attacked, he went to the barber's and got his hair cut, carefully, just a little, it didn't hurt, no, no blood, no, but if Sebastian gets attacked by one of those rabbits, a scissor rabbit, he may get his beautiful golden locks cut off and he'd look like those men in the street with no hair, you wouldn't like it, would you? no, who would? mommy? mommy's got a lot of hair, long hair, she's in no danger, she's not going with us hunting bears and rabbits, she's at work, making money so she can feed us, you and me, she'll be home later, yes, and we'll fix dinner for her and us because she'll be too tired to fix dinner after working all day, yes, she fixes it sometimes, especially on weekends because then she doesn't go to work, alight, it's time to stop now, daddy's tired and you too, no, yes you are, you just don't feel it, we'll stop hunting now and rest, fix ourselves lunch, yes and for Koko too, and for Moko whom we'll catch later, this afternoon, after your nap, yes, because he'll be very hungry from having lived in the woods so long and from being caught, because being caught makes you hungry, takes a lot out of you, that's why people, I mean bears, bears and rabbits don't like to be caught, nobody does, Sebastian wants an egg for lunch, the kind daddy makes cooking it slowly over boiling water, steam, stirring it all the time so that it comes out nice and creamy and delicious as if full of butter? yes? steam egg, eggs? steamed eggs? yes? yes, two for Sebastian and one for daddy, alright? two for Sebastian because he's growing, so that he'd grow big and strong, and one for daddy because he's grown already as far as he would, could, he doesn't want to grow any more, it'd be in the wrong direction, left and right and forwards and backwards, not up, he'd get fat, but Sebastian will grow in all directions, right and left and forwards and backwards and up and he'll be bigger, taller than daddy, real big and tall and will be able to fight off all that come to threaten him, him and mommy and daddy, fight off the night people, the ones that come at night and want to do harm to little boys and girls who sleep alone in their rooms, he'll be a warrior, a soldier, a soldier like daddy? no, daddy wasn't a soldier, he didn't want to be a soldier, to be commanded by anybody, told to do this and that, wanted to be left alone, to do his things, run and dream up stories like the ones he tells, but Sebastian will, Sebastian will be a soldier, like his grandfather I told you about, the one who was taken prisoner and escaped, dressed up as someone else, a high-ranked officer, and walked out through the camp gate as if nothing was the matter and was even saluted like an important person, a high-ranked officer, remember? yes? yes, the one who hid in a safe house for a while, then took a train with two other men to the mountains, where the border was and went through it illegally, in high mountains to another country, where he was safe and joined his family, us, he fell down a cliff? no, god forbid, he didn't, he nearly did, at night as they, the three of them, he and the other two men lay down to sleep, made themselves beds for the night, he made his bed against the trunk of a tree, and when he woke up in the morning there was a drop hundreds of feet down on the other side of the tree, and had he made just one more step in that direction he would have fallen down that precipice and gotten killed and I would have never seen him again, he was very lucky, and me too, and all of us, and you too? yes, you too even though you never saw him, because you were born after he died, went up there somewhere I told you about, because I wouldn't have had him to help me grow up and become a father to you, you see? it's all connected, we are what our parents and grandparents and so on have been and it continues like this forever, was he a great soldier? yes he was, he was a great soldier, a born soldier, that's all he could be, some people are like that, they can only be what they are born to be and when they become that they are very good at being, very good at being themselves, other people aren't meant for anything special and they become whatever life makes them, and then they are just so-so, nothing special, neither good nor bad, just nothing, but you will be big and strong and a soldier like your daddy, I mean your granddaddy, to fight off those bad people who try to break in at night to hurt you and mommy and daddy and Koko and Moko when we get him, which we will do after we eat and you take a nap and we fix the supper before mommy comes, right? yes, of course, yes, and you'll be like daddy too, run, and tell stories? yes, of course, you can be that also if you want to, if you try hard because it's hard to be all those things at the same time, but you can if you really want to, which probably means that you were meant to be like that, and some people are, it's amazing, and you won't fall off that cliff when you escape from the prison camp? no, of course not because you already know the precipice is there, because your granddaddy helped you, taught you, see, I told you, you were lucky too that he didn't fall off the cliff and made it to see his family, me because he told me about it and I told you, it's all interconnected, and you won't get caught by the police after you come off the mountains either, like one of his companions did as they were walking down the road and he went up ahead to reconnoitrer, to see if it was safe? no, of course not, because you'll know the police are there and you'll hide for a while until they pass, and there won't be any need for reconnoitering, checking if it's safe to walk on because you'll already know, because I've told you about what happened with your granddaddy, and you'll be an even better soldier than granddaddy? yes, in a way you will because he will have taught you through me what to do, how to be a better soldier, it's all interconnected as I said, and your feet won't be blistered from all that walking as his were when you get to the safe house as his were? well, we don't know about that, maybe they will or maybe they won't, maybe they won't if you wear better shoes so that your feet won't blister, it depends on that, so make sure you wear good shoes when you escape from that prison camp, but being in a prison camp, you don't have much choice what shoes you wear, you wear what you have, running shoes, like daddy's, the ones he wears when he goes running so that his feet won't blister? oh, yes, they'd be great but it's not

121

Yuriy Tarnawsky

likely you'd have them in the prison camp, you'd wear what you have, and your feet would probably blister but you'd still make it to that safe house, the second safe house, where they're expecting you, to get to your family, your son, to tell him about your escape so that he'd know what to do so as not to fall off a cliff and not get caught by the police and to wear running shoes when he escapes if he can so that his feet won't blister and be an even better soldier than you, it's all interconnected, you see?

16

THERE'S A MAN standing in the doorway, he's tall, thin, has sunken cheeks, sad eyes, staring down at me, looks old, who is he? my father? no, my father looked different, was smaller, smaller in old age, thinner and shorter, had gray hair, little of it, this one has lots, all black, a doctor? he's come to have a look at me? my wife was concerned about my situation, couldn't come, had to stay at the office, called a doctor, and asked him to go and see me and now he's standing there looking at me, deciding what to do? I was asleep, he saw that, stopped in the doorway, not sure what to do, wake me up or not? perhaps it'd be better not to wake me up so that I could rest up, gain strength, now that my eyes are open, he'll do something, will step up to the bed and ask me how I'm feeling, but no, it couldn't be, it couldn't be a doctor, how would he get in? the door is locked and he doesn't have a key, my wife couldn't have given hers to him, how? she couldn't have driven over and handed the key to him because she's as work, has to stay at the office, it would have been easier for her to come home and see me, she sent the key over by a messenger? that's crazy, no, too much trouble, where would she have found one? a messenger, very, very, extremely unlikely, no, the spare one? the spare key? the one we have hidden outside in the garden under a stone which we keep in case we lose ours so as not to have a locksmith come and break the lock? yes, it's possible but also unlikely, doctors don't make house calls any more and certainly don't go looking for keys under rocks in backyards, that's crazy too, no, not a doctor, or any other stranger, Sebastian? Sebastian then? my son? must be, must be him, looking old and unhappy, was married, his wife left him, ripped him off, and he's come to see me, to tell me what happened, to be consoled, helped, poor guy, poor man, poor men, women do it all the time to them, to good guys, to good, decent men, gold diggers they're called, the women, or just bitches, sluts, sluts all, poor Sebastian, my poor son, what he must have been through to look in the end like that, climbing walls like so many, so many men, although you can't say that women don't, they do too but not as many I think, and not for the same reason, the same way, men and women, the two sexes, are different, they laugh and cry differently, in different ways, for different reasons,

Sebastian? Sebastian? what is it? step up closer to the bed, closer to me, tell me, tell me what happened? how can I help you?, don't worry, it's not the end, there're plenty of other women in the world, good, decent women, loving women, plenty of fish in the sea, plenty of good, decent, loving women there somewhere, you'll find one in no time, in time, eventually, or she'll find you, you'll find each other, you've got to take your time, not to rush, not to get yourself into another mess again, on the rebound, with your looks you can have anybody, anyone, any girl you like, but take your time, relax, relax for now so that you don't make a mistake and have to go through the same mess again in a few years, enjoy life, enjoy yourself for yourself, for being yourself, for being, you don't need someone else to be happy, you've got to reach a point when you're happy with yourself, then you can be happy with others, only then, it's hard otherwise, it's hard to be happy with anyone as long as you're not happy with yourself, the other person will feel it, problems will arise and you'll be going through the same mess again, come, let's talk, tell me the stories I used to tell you when you were little, remember? about Flamino and Flamina, and The Magic Island, and the Good Fairy, and the four gnomes, Romo, Roro, Momo, and Moro, and the brave little mushroom called Ero, and the stupid dragon called Black Tooth, or about the dragon couple Iiiiiiiiii, and Iiii and their little son Ii and how Iiiiiiiiiii and Ii went hunting pots of sauerkraut soup and how one winter, when there was a lot of snow, Ii got lost in it and couldn't find himself because he was white and couldn't see himself in the snow until springtime, until spring came and the snow had all melted, or how we went hunting, you and I, in dark dense woods, hunting big bears and fierce rabbits, scissor rabbits, you riding on my shoulders and had to be careful the rabbits wouldn't cut off your beautiful golden locks because that's what they were after, they're black now and it looks like they are gray in places because you're much older and are going through tough times, no, you won't step up? because? because you're not Sebastian? you're not Sebastian? then who are you? me? you're me? the haggard-looking middle-aged man in the doorway is me standing in the door to my father's room where he died? where he died a day later, early morning, at six-thirty I think, and you, I mean I, one hundred and twenty miles away woke up screaming at that very instant from my throat closing up inside me so that I thought I'd choke, and they called me a couple of hours later to tell me he'd passed away and at that instant I knew that I already knew he did? so yes, I stood there twenty-four hours earlier in the door of the hospital room where he lay, having been urged to come as soon as possible because who knew how much longer he'd last, I having driven at break-neck speed, well, not at break-neck speed, being careful to make it there, to make sure I'd see him, not wanting him, his death to be the cause of mine, his death to be the cause of my not seeing him for the last time, so having driven as fast as safely as possible to make it there, to see him, having covered those one hundred and twenty miles in my car without stopping for a minute, second, I stood in the door of the hospital room he lay in, stood in the doorway not sure what to do, wait? step forward? turn around and walk away? because he didn't stir, stretched out on his back, his arms stretched out and crossed on his abdomen over the white sheet he was covered with, is he asleep? dead? alive? he didn't stir but looked alive, awake, staring with unfocused eyes into the ceiling, and I decided to go in, stepped up to the bed, him, said, Hi dad, how are you? touched his hand, he didn't stir, turn his head toward me, didn't shift his eyes, but went on staring into the ceiling, speaking immediately, obviously having recognized me, speaking about money, large sums, well, not really large, in fact pathetically small

127

sums, but many, many, that is number of them, words like "account, credit union, bank," and one word I didn't understand, couldn't figure out, which eventually turned out to be the name of a bank I never heard of, which he mispronounced, I tried to speak to him, stop him, find out how he was, but he went on, so I let him speak, went away, away from him, the bed, sat down in a chair against the wall facing he bed, watched, heard him speak, for a while, for a long time, he eventually beginning to stop for a while and then returning to speaking, the pauses getting progressively longer and longer and periods of speaking shorter and shorter, I not trying to interrupt him, to speak to him, sure it wouldn't work, letting him go on, letting him go on dying, with time noticing my cheekbones, my cheeks were wet, realizing that tears were streaming out of my eyes, quietly, without sobs, without particular feeling, emotion, by themselves, like urine leaking out of a bladder over which control has been lost, I remembering him young, handsome, strong, running down the hallway, from room to room with me on his shoulders, legs along his chest, ankles in his hands, telling me how he was being careful not to run into that tree, that rock up ahead where the path curved, through dark woods, hunting big bears and fierce rabbits, couldn't explain to the nurse why I was crying, He's fine, she said, He'll be fine, but I said, No, he isn't, I'll never see him again, and when they said I had to leave, I came up to the bed, bent down, kissed his hand, don't remember which, probably the left one, closer to me, I being on the left side of him, the bed, moved over to the right, kissed his cheek, left one for sure, remember now, still bending down, said, I love you, dad, straightened up, looked at him one more time, his forehead, the skull big and round, its shape threatened but not misshaped by the encroaching pillow, and without his speaking left, not turning around in the doorway for the last look.

17

TUS VEINTE AÑOS *temblando de cariño bajo el beso que* *entonces te robé,* did I kiss her? I must have, yes, I did, her unexpecting, parting lips, moisture, coolness inside them, the smoothness of her teeth beyond scared me, god, what have I done? what am I doing? she's so defenseless, innocent, a flower, a flower I stepped on, I crushed the flower of her lips, how dare I? what is she going to do? slap my face? scream for help? police? I wouldn't blame her, I took my hands off her face, turned around, and ran, *al llegar al terraplén?* no, not at *terraplén*, not at the embarkment, past the big wall, far away from the hardware store corner, her sidewalk, home, window, not in the *barrio*, Pompea, Buenos Aires, that, Buenos Aires, was later, more about it later, this was in that square with the famous huge cast iron fountain always playing its beautiful deaf-mute sign water music, by the famous old gate that's no longer there, in K, Kk, Kr, Kra, Krakow? No, not in Krakow, that was also later, this was in that other city, Q, Que, Cue, Cue Gardens, Kew Gardens?

no, something Ku, Kw, Kwe, can't remember, strange, it's important, it's an important city, important to me, in my life, it's strange I can't remember its name, it tells you the state I'm in, but it's alright, it doesn't matter, it will come back, it will come back eventually, anyway, I ran down the steps, then the long escalator to the subway station down below, took the train, ran up the long, long escalator onto the street, down the street to the apartment building, into the elevator, up to the third floor, into the apartment, got a pen, paper, sat at the round dining room table, penned a letter, purple, blue, no delicate lilac on white, begging to be excused pardoned, I couldn't help it, I love you, got a stamp, envelope, sealed it, wrote down the address she gave me, where she was going to be, hers, her parents' home where she lived, ran out, dropped the letter in the mailbox in the street, not wanting to waste a minute, second, to make sure not to miss the morning, eight-thirty pickup, went to sleep, next morning, in the next morning's mail there was a letter from her written before she went away, before we met in that square, before I kissed her, she not knowing we would meet, it said, I love you, wait for me, I will be back, I kissed it, cried, there is god! two days later, as I was trying to hide, bending down behind the bodies of those before me, the priest did manage to reach me with the holy, blessed water, as if throwing a handful of ice-cold kernels of transparent wheat all over me, laughing cheerfully, Did you think you could escape god's blessing? and that evening at dusk, I was scared for a moment I wouldn't be able to find my way out of the lilac bushes blooming with their pale lilac color like I've never seen before or imagined existed, being of exactly the same color myself inside, and the *lunas suburbanas*, yes, they were there, except later, much, that is somewhat later, and not *lunas* except *luna*, a moon, and *urbanas* rather than *sub*, a huge full white moon as we wended our way down the winding path, paths along the steep slope, slopes between and under the dense leafy trees, she holding her huge white pregnant belly and the balloon above it with her white hands with me next to her, my hands trembling, making sure she wouldn't stumble, fall down, damage, unmake the precious fruit inside her, the moon helping along, doing what it could from that distance and through the gaps between the dense black leaves, but below much more, helping out much more in the huge river with mist rising above its water looking like a giant, enormous peasant bed, its linen all messed up, messed up during the night and left unmade since the morning, she and I too, all of us stepped into it, moving slowly, the water cold on our skin although warmer than the air, the long white dresses, shirts I mean, rising along the women's bodies like big white wreaths, they, the women, holding onto their big bellies, the balloons under the cloth, fabric pressed to their midriffs, until the wreaths, the water was above their breasts, almost up to their chins, and then they, the women, released them, the balloons, helping them wiggle their way out from under the fabric into the open, liberate themselves from under their chins, and rise free into the silvery sky, their bodies white, the strings on the end wiggling like the tails of so many spermatozoa, sperms with the sole aim of impregnating the giant white egg of the moon in the zenith, but as was said, Buenos Aires was there too, I don't know how much, how many years later, five? seven? but not the *barrio*, not Pompea, pretty much in the center, a small hotel not far from the parliament, and the *Casa Rosada* for that matter, shabby, nondescript, uninteresting, I mean Buenos Aires, not the hotel, shabby, nondescript, uninteresting, although the hotel not particularly interesting either, so Buenos Aires once again, shabby, nondescript, uninteresting stuffy and muggy in its early fall, our early spring, Café Tortoni for lunch or dinner, heard the tango Sur performed, sung once, stood on the *esquina* San Juan and

Boedo Antigua, good *reserva* red wine in the afternoons, the sun coming in through the window on the right falling onto her bare Henry Moore sculpture back below me at the distance of my outstretched arms.

18

SEBASTIAN! SEBASTIAN! COME here! stop digging in the ground! you're all dirty, hands, fingers, mouth, it's all over your face, mouth, god! what are you chewing on, eating? meat? what kind of meat? where did you get it? it came by itself? what do you mean it came by itself? somebody gave it to you? no? so how did it come by itself? crawling? the meat crawling? show it to me! spit it out! here, spit it out! god, it's an earthworm! Sebastian, what am I going to do with you? spit it out! all of it out! all! spit! not in my hand, on the ground, spit! spit! more, more, you can't? alright, here, take a sip, don't swallow it, just keep it in your mouth and swish it around like when you brush your teeth, yes, but spit it out, don't swallow it, don't swallow it, spit! alright, god! what am going to do with you? I hope it's not poisonous, the earthworm, I don't think they are, the earthworms, I don't think they are poisonous, I hope not, if you're sick, if you feel sick, sick to the stomach, tell me right away, OK? we'll have to see a doctor, go to the hospital if you do, god, Sebastian, you're such a pain, I don't know what I'm going to do with you, here, take a swig and rinse your mouth with it, and then spit it out once more, don't swallow it, alright, now one more time, drink, swish it around, alright, swish it around some more, now spit it out, alright, good, how does it feel inside? clean? yes? alright, how did it taste? not the water but what you ate, the meat that came along by itself? good? like what daddy makes for supper? god! you're something else, Sebastian! what am I going to do with you? I think I'll go to work and have mommy stay home and take care of you, would you prefer that? yes? no? maybe? you don't know? here, let me wash off your face, careful, close your mouth and eyes, keep them closed, god! let me wipe you off, god! my handkerchief's all dirty now and wet, here, some more, wait, wait, let me dry you off well, you'll have to take a bath when we come home, alright, now your hands, stick them out and keep close together, like that, yes, alright, good, now rub them together, rub well! some more! now some water, rub! rub well! rub some more! it's alright for now, I'll have to give you a good wash when we get home, here, dry your hands off on the handkerchief, I know it's wet but it's drier along the edges, over here, yes, some more,   alright now, but remember, no digging in the ground and no eating meat that comes along by itself, it's not meat but worms, it was a rainworm, an earthworm you ate, he lives in the ground and comes out when it rains, it looks like meat, red, but it isn't, it's full of clay inside, it eats clay as it moves along and passes it and that's why it can travel through the soil, earth, did you swallow it? yes? just a little? good, maybe it won't hurt you, it probably won't, but we'll have to watch you and if you're sick you'll have to see the doctor, you like to see the doctor? candy? candy's bad for you, I don't know why they have it for kids at the doctor's office when they know it's bad, probably to lure them in, to make sure they don't refuse, that they like to come, but still, anyway, so how did it taste, the meat that came out of the ground by itself, the worm? good? you liked it? like what daddy fixes for supper? my god, Sebastian, you're terrible, is my cooking really that bad? yes? no? maybe? no? maybe I'll go to work after all and have mommy stay home and take care of you, no? why not? because my cooking's better? no? hers is better? the same? good? better because of the sweet omelets? alright, but my cooking's good otherwise, right? better? better otherwise because of the tomato soup? alright, but otherwise the cooking of both of us is good, yes? alright, but why do you prefer for mommy to work and daddy stay home and take care of you? because mommy doesn't gallop?

139

doesn't gallop with you on her shoulders? I see, well, that's a good reason, I agree, and doesn't go hunting with you in the dark woods? big bears and fierce rabbits? that's an even better reason, I agree, and no stories? she does tell you stories, doesn't she? short? too short? and not so much fun? not dark? what do you mean, not dark? not about scary things? not about people that come to hurt little children asleep in their beds at night? but I don't tell you such stories, no, not at night? because she doesn't tell her stories at night? but I don't tell you my stories at night only, I also tell them in the daytime, so what do you mean, not dark? that things I tell you about happen at night? but some of the things I tell you happen in the daytime too, but my stories are still dark? yes? why? because they're like when you close your eyes? oh, I see, that's nice, like when you close your eyes, that's wonderful, that's what they're supposed to be, and you like them? yes? that's good, that's great, you're the boss here, you decide what you like and what you call it, everyone does, that's called freedom and everybody has a right to it and other people have to accept it, and daddy accepts yours, and he'll stay with you and take care of you while mommy works and will tell you all the dark stories you want to hear, good, so now we've agreed on it, fine, but you mustn't dig in the ground and eat meat that's there, eat worms while daddy's not looking, alright? you mustn't do it regardless of whether daddy's looking or not, you're hungry? alright, we can have our sandwiches now, good, we'll sit at the table over there, fine, here's yours and this is mine, yours is smaller, you want to have the big one, alright, but you must finish it, alright? you will? are you sure? last week you couldn't finish it and we fed it to the fish, you were full? that's fine but you mustn't ask for more than what you can eat, you will eat it all today? you're sure? alright, it's because this one is with tuna fish salad and the other one was with peanut butter and jelly? yes? and you weren't hungry for peanut butter and jelly but you will be for tuna fish salad? because it's so good? because daddy makes tuna fish salad best? better than mommy? that's because it was his invention and he taught mommy to make it, but it's hard to make something better than the person who's invented it, sometimes it happens, but it's very seldom, alright, you can have the big one and I'll have the small one, and you'll have your milk, and I water, what's left of it, milk? no, no milk, daddy likes milk but he's been gaining weight lately and milk's too caloric, has too much fat, he has to watch what he eats, milk will make him grow fat, big, yes, he's not fat yet but he will

141

be if he eats too much and drinks milk, so, you eating his sandwich and he eating yours is good, is good for him, he won't get fat this way, run? he likes to run but he doesn't have enough time, he can't go running and leave you alone in the house, would you like it if he went running for an hour and you stayed alone in the house? no? no, he runs some on weekends and other times when mommy's at home and sometimes at night after mommy's back from work, you don't mind it then, do you? no, why should you? but daddy can't run as much as he used to, his knee hurts, he ran too much for many years and hurt his knee, so now he has to be careful about not running too much, galloping in the house with you on his shoulders hurting his knee? no, it doesn't make his knee hurt, he can do it with no problem, later, when we finish eating? yes, we will walk in the woods along the lake, but no galloping, too dangerous, it's too dangerous there, there are rocks and tree roots there on the path and if daddy would catch his toe on one of them and he'd fall down and you with him, whoaaa! a real bad fall, especially for you way up there on my shoulders, you'd go flying like I don't know what, a bird, way down the path, might get hurt, break off your beautiful golden locks and then some more, you wouldn't want that, would you? you'd look then like those

men you see in the streets who'd been attacked by fierce
scissor rabbits and have no hair on their heads, no, of course
you wouldn't, daddy's locks? they're not that long and there
aren't that many of them left, so perhaps they wouldn't be
broken off that much, and he wouldn't go flying as far as you
because he'd be closer to the ground, no, no galloping and
no bear and fierce rabbit hunting, we'll just stroll along the
path along the lake and come back to the car, eat on, eat on,
how's the sandwich? will you finish it? yes? for sure? want
some of mine? yes? god, Sebastian, you have no manners,
you have to be polite and show consideration for others,
other people's needs and feelings, everyone gets hungry
and you have to be mindful of that, I'm hungry too and you
can't have mine and some of originally your sandwich, I drink
your milk? no, I will drink my water and eat my sandwich,
which was originally yours, and you will drink you milk and
eat your sandwich which was originally mine and then we'll
go for a walk along the lake, too bad it's not early spring and
some ten years earlier, you would have seen some beautiful
swanlings, baby swans on the lake, you remember the
swans we saw on the lake in the park in the city last year?
the geese that have real long necks? like in the story about
the ugly duckling? yes, exactly, I forgot I'd read the story to

you, well they, the little swans, they were so beautiful, gray
with shiny-shiny black beaks, even though their parents,
mother and father were snow-white, like the Snow White with
the seven dwarfs? no, she wasn't white as snow, she was
just called that, the swans were white like the snow the little
dragon li got lost in, like he himself, you understand? yes?
like milk? yes, like milk, drink it up, you like the sandwich?
yes? will finish it? yes? good, daddy will finish his too,
alright, well the parents, the father and the mother, the two
big swans would come up from the south every spring, late
February or early March, she, the mother would build herself
a big nest out of twigs over there in the reeds and bushes at
the end of the lake, lay eggs and hatch them, sit on them for
a long time, two-three weeks, maybe a month until they
hatched, until the little ones hatched and came out of the
eggshells, like baby chicks? yes, like the baby chicks we
saw at the big store that sells Christmas trees, where we get
our Christmas tree and they have the little zoo for kids like
you, that's right, so the father, the male swan stuck around
too, making sure no one would hurt her, the mother swan,
and would take her place in the nest when she would go and
eat, why? to keep the eggs warm, so that they wouldn't go
bad and not hatch, so you could see this white spot among

the reeds and bushes, her and sometimes him, for a long time, maybe a month, and then one day it'd be gone, and you'd see her swimming in the middle of the lake, her beautiful long white neck curving, with these little gray things behind her, the little baby swans, swanlings, like the wake, a wave she was leaving behind as she swam, play with them? no, they wouldn't play with children because they're wild, but sometimes they'd all, the little ones and the mother would come up to the shore and wait for you to throw them some bread to eat, they'd stay on the lake all summer until late fall and then they'd fly off south for the winter, the little ones would grow big like the parents and white too, so that in the end you almost couldn't tell them apart, and when spring came, the two old ones would come back and have another batch of little ones again, the little ones? the young ones? the children? they died? I don't think so, they probably found new lakes for themselves or something, I don't know why they didn't come here, maybe this lake is too small, it's not very big, I don't know, but the parents, the old swans, they liked it and kept coming back, until eventually they stopped and no swans come here any more, died? did they die? they probably did, swans don't live that long, I don't know how long they live but I'm sure not as long as people, not as long as mommy and daddy and you, no, why don't other swans come here any more? as I told you, I don't know, probably because there aren't that many of them left, not as many little ones hatch each year, why? why not as many? there're pesticides, bad things, poison in the food they eat, the grass, weeds, whatever, and that makes the eggs unfertile, so that they don't hatch, the little ones don't come out, the old swans, they used to have three babies every year for a long time, and then there were just two for a while, and finally one, I think for two years, and then none for another two. and then the swans stopped coming, they either died or gave up, saw no point in coming back, it's like this with all creatures, they're having fewer and fewer children, bad food and stress, everything changing, getting worse, babies don't want to be born any more, but you did? yes, you did, you did.

19

THE DOOR EMPTY again, why do I keep looking there all the time, fidgeting as if being uncomfortable? must be expecting someone, my wife? home from work? no, it's too early for that, for her to come, she comes around five-thirty and I'm sure it's not that late, must be three-thirty-four, four-thirty at the latest, or maybe closer to five, four-forty-five, but not five-thirty,anyway, she always calls before leaving, around five-five, after five or so, or almost always, I urge her to call so that I know when to expect her, so that I won't worry something happened to her on the way home, especially in that one spot where the cars come speeding in from the right, from the other highway, and she has to turn right herself like about a hundred feet farther down, they go left and she goes right and they speed like crazy, a real dangerous spot, they should do something about it, have a yield sign for those cars so that they slow down because they come barreling down like they're the only ones there, like they own the damn road, whereas they're coming in and

Yuriy Tarnawsky

there's more traffic on the road they're coming onto than on the one they're on, I get upset when she doesn't call and isn't home at five-thirty or a little later, five-thirty-five, quarter to six, start fidgeting around with this uneasy feeling in me as if I'm stuck in a closed space, a real tight culvert I can't even move in with the end barely in sight, overcome by an attack of claustrophobia which I have and have it badly, visions of her car smashed at that merge place, the metal, steel of the chassis and the aluminum or whatever the body, the car body is made of intermixed with her, hers, don't want to say that frightening word, those frightening words, god! too grizzly to even permit myself to think about it, let alone think or god forbid speak, side effects, effects, scars, whatever of abandonment, of total, well, near-total, you can never have total, abandonment at an early, most vulnerable age, ten years, as always, a mark, impact, in this case head-on impact, on a person's personality, life, although genetic factors can't be fully excluded here, after all we're nothing but genes, and what dents a sheet of aluminum will not leave a mark on a steel plate, anyway, it's not that time and I'm sure she'll call before leaving, and I don't have to start worrying why she's late before she is, before she leaves work, waiting for? waiting for a man of course, a young man, dark, slender handsome, handsome to me of course, handsomeness is a relative term, a marked quality, like a fat woman being a beautiful mama because she's your mother and you've grown up, fed on milk from her breast, waiting of course for Sebastian, my son, he's gone out on an errand to get something, something for himself and/or me, a pack of cigarettes or chewing gum for himself or a drink of some kind and/or medicine for me, no, no cigarettes for him, he doesn't smoke, none in my family did except my father, his grandfather who was a chain smoker until the age of forty-five or so, after he got back from that prison camp, after he found us, and the veins in his right leg were plugged up with nicotine from too much smoking, or maybe not plugged up but cramped up, shriveled up so that he could barely walk a few hundred yards before he'd have to stop, doubled up with pain, and he had an operation, cutting of nerves, to permit the other, side veins pump enough blood, Bergman's or Berger's disease I think it's called, something like that, no, that's wrong, Berger's disease has something to do with kidneys, it's something else starting with a "B" I think, can't remember now, too many years, too long ago, anyway, so when he recovered, he stopped smoking altogether, with no help, no drugs, one day, cold turkey, that's willpower for you, character, he was some man, someone to model yourself on, which I tried, yes, anyway Sebastian's out to get something for himself or me or both, an electrolyte drink for me, for instance, should be back soon, what do I mean soon? he's been away for a while, I've been waiting for him for a long time, he's not out on an errand, he hasn't arrived yet, lives far away, in that distant god-forsaken city, town, far away, in the middle of nowhere, they let him know, my wife, his mother let him know I'm in bad shape and he should come as soon as possible if he wants to see me, I mean speak to me, see me alive, so he's taking the train, he still doesn't have a car, it's still summer, a few months after he moved there, got the job, has to save up enough money to buy a car, learn how to drive, take a driving course, a cab to the station, or a walk, it's not that far away, a few long blocks along those empty god-forsaken streets, I mean empty streets through the near-abandoned industrial quarter, then along the wide new road down the open incline, I mean the area they cleaned up after raising the abandoned factories, and breweries, and warehouses, laid a broad clean road, a park, an empty area with a few small trees, so down the open incline to the station, wait for the train, late as always, then the ride, two, no three hours I think, then a cab or a bus to the hospital, should be here any minute, second, the nurse will bring him in, no, god, what am I saying? not to the hospital, I'm not in a hospital, I'm at home, and I don't think he's in that far-away god-forsaken city, town either, not any longer, and never was, I think, I think it was me, and my wife, his mother wouldn't leave me alone if I was in that bad a shape, near dying, she wouldn't be at work while I was alone in the house on the verge of dying, so no, he's not coming, I mean he's not coming from far away, I think he lives with us, taking care of me while my wife, his mother works to support both of us, I mean the three of us, or maybe no, maybe she's not, maybe she's abandoned us both, both of us, is far away, alone, with her family or married to someone else, women do that, like to do that, drop their man and find a better provider, better, sweeter sugar daddy, or maybe more, or less, or better, or different sex, although that's not often the case, couldn't, wouldn't be the case here, and it's not, my wife lives with me, we live together, she's at work, working to support us, to supplement my meager pension so that we'd live better, more comfortably, better food, wine, travel, vacations, he, my son, Sebastien just drops in sometimes, often, on a regular basis, single, busy with his own things, matter of the heart and the crotch, mostly crotch most

Yuriy Tarnawsky

probably, men are like that, more like that than women, genes, biology most likely, almost definitely so, biologically speaking man is a device created for procreation, sire offspring, sire as many offspring as possible, no, I should have said, man is a device that's trying to survive in spite of being mortal, feeding yourself, staying healthy, trying to live as long as possible is one tack, but that one is a dead end in the end, literally dead end, you'll die, it's certain even if you do all you can, stand on your head etc., in the end you'll die, no one gets out alive out of this trap, so you try to prolong yourself, have a try at being immortal by procreating, by producing creatures, devices that carry your genes, only half of yours, that's true, but it's better than nothing, zero, half, fifty percent is better than zero, hell of a lot better, infinitely better if you resort to mathematics, arithmetic, although there's a rule, law against dividing by zero, but you can do it in the privacy of your home, mind, under the covers, in the darkness, in the darkness of your mind, so you want, try to have offspring, children, at least a child but potentially many, the more the better, more chances of survival, of having a shot at eternity, as an oak tree drops its myriad, well many hundreds, perhaps a few thousands acorns so that some that sprout shoots take root, grow into trees, dandelions do the same by sending off their dozens of parachutes, little air travelers trying to prolong their mother's/father's life, to prolong themselves, hell, why do I have to resort to dandelions? men's sperm, spermatozoa do the same, travel like crazy forward down the dark channel, corridor of the vagina and then even darker pitch-black culvert, pipe of the womb toward the bright light of the egg, ovum at the end, well, a man can impregnate thousands of women but a woman can be impregnated only once every nine months, a year actually or even more if you count what she and her body, that is, she as a person and her body as a device have to go through to nurture a child before bringing another one into this world, both want the offspring to be as good as possible, as potentially successful a procreational device as possible, but men have more leeway, more chances, cast their seed into many fertile soils, onto wider ground, like oak trees and dandelions, women must be careful, they can succeed only once every year or so, or as I said even more than a year, select the best specimen, best not only in its makeup, genes but also as a mate, partner in bringing up the child, provider, protector, insurer of the offspring's future, so it's different for both, different for men and women, although of course there're exceptions, women who are promiscuous, sleep around, they're called nymphomaniacs, something's wrong with them, a form of neurosis, something in their life that changed them, a deep psychological wound, at least that's what I think, but who am I to know everything, anyway and of course there are men who overdo it too, ladies' men they're called, skirt chasers, philanderers, but in general it's more natural, it's natural, I mean, it's the normal call of the genes, sperm, spermatozoa, a loud call you may ignore but can't avoid hearing as a man, so as a man you primarily chase one woman at a time but may have another one in mind, lined up for when you're ready, and he's like that, he's chasing one or more prospects, possibilities of procreation, so he, my son, Sebastian, he's busy, busy with the things he's supposed to be busy with, lives with us, his mother and me, has stepped out on an errand to get something, something for me, medicine or a drink, an electrolyte drink or something, or/and something for himself too, got distracted by something to do with his primary obligation, primary function, the function of procreation, need to procreate, is temporarily busy with the act, with affairs of the heart and the crutch, crutch mostly and most probably, will be back soon, back any moment, I must be patient, I must wait.

20

WHAT WAS IT, moon? balloon? balloon moon? moon balloon? the moon like a balloon? a balloon like the moon? a full moon? a giant full white moon? a pregnant belly like a full moon? a white balloon like a pregnant belly? something like that, women clutching big white balloons under their shirts like pregnant bellies or over pregnant bellies, balloons freed from under shirts and chins streaming toward the moon high up in the sky like sperm, spermatozoa toward an egg in the womb, yes, it was something like that, must have been something like that, women up to their chins in water, men and women intermixed up to their chins in water, also in a field, in a clearing in a forest, men and women intermixed in a circle around a bonfire, in separate circles around bonfires, women inside, men outside, separate side-by-side circles rotating in the same, opposite directions around bonfires, white balloons, their strings wiggling like the tails, flagella of vigorous spermatozoa streaming up toward the full moon high up in the sky, some sort of a ritual, a modern-day game of city people imitating an old pagan, folk, Indo-European, East European, Slavic most probably folk ritual, yes, a Slavic folk ritual of bathing in the river in late spring, early summer, later, dancing in a forest clearing around a bonfire at night, to promote fertility and health of the fetus, yes, I think there were both pregnant and unpregnant women, girls, females there, clutching white balloons, the unpregnant ones white balloons, the pregnant ones bellies and white balloons which, released, looked like vigorous spermatozoa with their flagella wigging as they streamed, rose toward the moon way high up in the clear sky, but also a white balloon that the little retarded Down Syndrome boy, the son of the superintendent ran around with in the courtyard of the building we lived in, pointing, stabbing with his sharp little finger at the sky, calling out all the time, Huh, huh, huh, huh, huh! and his father, old, must have been in his sixties, saying, No, Oscar, no! No, Oscar, no! No, Oscar, no! Oscar! Oscar! Oscar! No, no, no! Oscar and not Sebastian? hmmm, not sure, Oscar more likely, but possibly Sebastian, yes, possibly Sebastian, he, the father barely looking up, that is seldom looking up as he toiled, bent down over something, cleaning up or fixing something, carrying out his superintendent's duties, his pale bald head, pate shiny with perspiration, looked like a retired professor working to supplement his meager pension rather than a superintendent, with his gold-rimmed glasses, spectacles, and his fine-featured face of an intellectual, always wearing that black vest, unbuttoned, over his white shirt, its sleeves rolled up above the elbows, suspenders underneath supporting his baggy worn black pants, his Charlie Chapin pants the balloon got away from the boy, headed first this way and then that low above the ground, not sure which way to go, this time not looking like anything other than a balloon that's lost its way, the boy went crazy with his, Huh, huh, huh, huh, huh! stabbing at the sky, in the direction of the balloon, the father, the professor-superintendent seeing too late what had happened, ran after it for a few paces before stopping and giving up, there was clearly no point, no point wasting his energy, watching with helplessness as the wind caught it and carried it up, then a little sideways, close to me, closer to me on the balcony, closer to the balcony where I stood, I reached out with my hand barely trying, knowing it wouldn't get close enough, knowing I couldn't catch it because it wasn't going to come close enough to me, then watched it float, rise vertically higher and higher past the red-tiled roofs of the buildings, the dark crowns, tops of the giant trees that grow everywhere there, past the massive high-rises with their cluttered or glassed-in balconies, into the empty pale blue sky, its string dead limp like a spent, sterile sperm's tail, flagellum, also perhaps because there was no moon, no egg for it to go for, went inside and lay down on the leather sofa in the living/dining room, pale green light from the lush trees outside on all sides, all around, silence, stillness, lots of walls, it seemed like nothing but walls, plane surfaces all around me, dozens and dozens, hundreds and hundreds of plane surfaces, up front, in the back, on the right, on the left, above, below, that's what's always around us, always, from the beginning to the very end, especially the end, walls, nothing but walls, six to be precise at the end, six forever, bad number, that six, stay away from it, we have 666, Antichrist, the devil, no wonder, but where was she? working? no, she didn't work then, later, much later, out shopping, to get something in that little corner grocery/liquor store across the street, outside the compound? bread? milk? wine? no, that was later too, she wasn't there yet, I was waiting for her, that's it, I was waiting for her the first time, and then she came, and then there was that ritual she heard about from a friend of hers, a fellow student, just a friend, not a boyfriend, a potential girlfriend of his told him about it, about the ritual, invited him to participate, to participate in a ritual on the river at night, of girls wearing wreaths with lit candles on their heads and setting them on water, in the river, of men catching the wreaths, and later, later that day, I mean, night, dancing and singing about couples and marriage in a clearing in the woods around bonfires, and jumping over flames while holding hands, yes, and the moon and the balloon was later, was a year or two later, maybe twice, once with just the balloon and then with the belly and the balloon, a year apart, I think, yes, a year apart, on that holiday, the holiday devoted to that deity, the deity of fertility, yes, one perhaps in the clearing and one in the river, the water, yes, that's it, for sure, a year apart, with a full moon, on the day devoted to that deity, on the hills and in the river, but in different places, each of the three rituals at the same day, but in different places, first the one with wreaths and candles and bonfires, and the second one in a clearing, with bonfires and balloons streaming spermatozoa-like skyward in an act of hope, in an *auto da fé*, a sui generis *auto da fé*, and the third in the water, in the river, except not stark naked, but dressed, wearing clothes, the same clothes, I mean clothes like on the other occasions, like the year before and the one before that, clothes similar, but not the same, yes, that's it, yes, but the little boy, the retarded Oscar-Sebastian was running around too, right? yes, he was, and we worried, worried because of my age, because of my age? because of my age maybe a little, my age wasn't that bad, not as bad as his, the boy's retired professor-janitor father's, so we mostly just worried when we thought she was pregnant, when her belly started to bulge, bulged a little, we worried it'd be as with the boy, and we contacted for the third time them, the people, because they organized, ran all three events, rituals, and that night before midnight, at eleven-thirty perhaps, we sneaked out of the apartment, hiding the key in the usual spot behind a loose brick in the wall, dressed as we were told, in the clothes we were provided as always, she in a loose calf-length shirt of coarse home-spun linen, I in a similar shorter shirt and pants with legs a bit too short and too tight for me, but barefoot, both of us barefoot, raincoats over ourselves, long raincoats, to hide the clothes we wore, she with a balloon, a big white balloon in a plastic bag in her hand which continually tried to free itself, to get away, to rise up in the sky, eager like a nervous horse anxious to do its duty, walked to the nearby park, past the little corner grocery/liquor store, down the empty, barely lit street, past the huge government building on the left, black, blacker than usual, built out of enormous gray granite blocks that turned black at night like lights that'd gone out, into the park, down the broad alleys, past the government palace, and into the woods that stretched along the ridge, parallel to the river, dark, dense, as if in the middle of nowhere, I checked the moon as we came into a little clearing among the trees, it was there, tiny it seemed in the small hole between the tops of the trees although it looked giant seen from another spot a little later above the land, we took our raincoats off, stuck them into the plastic bag, hid it in the bushes, she pushed the balloon under her shirt over her belly which we thought was possibly bulging already, which may have already bulged a little, and then treaded gingerly along the well-trodden path, paths, the clay under the soles of our feet still moist and slippery from the afternoon rain, light afternoon rain, I on the left, she on the right, clutching her hand to make sure she wouldn't slip and fall and hurt herself, hurt the possible precious cargo, the possible precious fruit inside her, or if not it, if not the fruit, then herself, so that she wouldn't fall down and hurt herself and not be able to carry the fruit inside her nine months or a year or so, whatever, later, it was real slippery going down along the slope, and I nearly fell down myself a few times, so worried constantly about her, but in the end, finally we found ourselves sound and safe down below, by the river, with some couples already there standing, waiting, others emerging here and there from among the woods, the moon as I said much, much bigger now with the land below for comparison, we all huddled, crowded for a while, not chatting, not saying anything, so as not to break the magic, the charm of the ritual, and then upon a whispered command, silently, slowly moved toward the water, each couple holding hands, in a crowd, not in a circle like in the woods that first time earlier and then the second one a year later, the water at first cold but gradually not warm but also no longer chilling, neutral, as if part of ourselves, our bodies, along my legs, rising along my legs, belly, chest, up, up, way up, almost to the chin, almost up to my chin, it was quiet all around, just the now near, now distant lisp of the water, we looked up, the moon seemed smaller, higher up, in the zenith, and suddenly one, then another, then still another, and more and more balloons were seen rising into the air and I turned to her, the water was way up to her chin, the cloth of her shirt pressed against it, chocking her, her eyes bulging, the shirt pressed up by the bulging pregnant body of the balloon, our hands working together, we helped it get out and it rose, freeing her, finally free itself, happy and grateful into the sky, it seemed, in the direction of the moon, its string, a sperm tail, a spermatozoa flagellum wiggling gradually more and more vigorously.

21

BUT WAIT, WASN'T there a Sebastian, a horse named
Sebastian that father rode when we lived at that count's
estate when I was little, a beautiful white stallion always
dancing and prancing unable to stand still, its neck curved
like that of a giant muscular swan, no, that's not right, swans
can't be muscular, a muscular swan would look like a horse,
his, the Sebastian horse's neck curved like the head of a
beautiful eighteenth century Italian violin, its white body
rippling with muscles under the skin like a huge current of
milk coming out of an opening under high pressure, no, I'm
wrong again, father's horse wasn't white but dappled,
beautiful dappled white and gray, and it was called Jan, Jan
something, wait, wait, Amor, Jan Amor, yes it was called Jan
Amor, Jan Love, yes, Jan Love for a good reasons, and it did
dance and prance trying to go forward and backward and
sideways, unable to stand still, father in the saddle up on his
back tall like a church steeple, yes, he did that during the
funeral, during the funeral of the countess, the count's wife,

riding in front of the procession, always sideways, now the left forward, now the right, no, I'm crazy, of course it wasn't at the funeral, you never have a rider riding a horse at the head of a funeral procession, it's not a wedding or something, you have nothing in front of a funeral procession except maybe a brass band marching on foot playing it's black music, it's music like blasts of soot belching out of the tubas, and trumpets, and whatever else those instruments are called, Chopin's Funeral March or something else sad and slow, something by Berlioz, don't know, maybe a jazz composition, and this time, at the countess' funeral, yes, there was a brass band marching at the head of the cortege while playing, playing Chopin's Funeral March most probably, then came the hearse with a black silver-fringed canopy supported by four fluted posts with the coffin on it, drawn by a pair, a pair? no, not two, four, or was it six? no, only four, I remember now, four black horses with what looked like bouquets of black feathers on their heads, quiet, placid, not stallions but beautiful, solemn, like four widows marching together each having lost her own, separate husband, and further down behind the count and his family came we, father, mother, and I, I between them, they holding my hands, father on the left, mother on the right, I in the middle, and that day, not the funeral day, another one, before the funeral, I think, yes, before the funeral, when father took me up on that beautiful white stallion of his, called Sebastian, god, no, what am I saying again? what is the matter with me? why this white horse all the time? I've just said father's horse was called Jan Amor, not Sebastian, and it wasn't white but dappled, a beautiful white and gray dappled, yes, it was a stallion, but I didn't ride with him on it often, just once, it was too dangerous, they said, the horse was too spunky, unpredictable, a boy riding with his father could be easily thrown off it and injured or, god forbid, killed, but that day again, morning, early, well, more like mid-late spring or early summer morning, late May/early June, I was playing in the black currant bushes in front of the house we lived in and heard the clanking, whooshing of horse hooves on the gravel road, or better, pathway that ran past the house and then curved sharply to the left a little farther on and eventually ran past the big building, the manor house, right by it, under the portico, for carriages and automobiles to ride through, it sounded like it was many horses, not just one, so, intrigued, I ran out from the bushes and saw father and that young woman father worked with that mother didn't like, a relative of the count, I think, who lived on the estate, in the manor house, Anela or Adela, I think she was called, Adela, I think, yes, Miss Adela, father on Jan Amor and she on the countess' little white mare, Marissa or/no not Marissa, Marysia, yes, Marysia, she often rode to exercise her because the countess was too sick to do it, she never stepped out of the house any longer then, as I recall, father in a brown jacket, his mustard-colored riding britches, and black boots, and Miss Adela in a white shirt and tight black pants and boots, they were coming back from inspecting something being done in the fields, and I ran out onto the middle of the pathway and Jan Amor danced up to me sideways as he sometimes did, and I asked father, Take me up on the horse, and he didn't say no as he always did but came close to me sideways on the horse, on the left, and bent way down, and lifted me up real quickly, as if by magic, a magic, magnetic force inside him, and sat up straight in the saddle, and held me up in his arms, and I saw the world from there as if from high up in a tree, its top, or even higher, a bell tower, a belfry towering over the church and the world around it, our house, the pathway, the green lawn along it that separated the building we lived in from the manor house, smooth as a billiard table, like the one the count and father played on in one of the rooms in the manor house, and felt a joy I don't think I ever felt again, certainly not before, he held me up there for a while, so that I'd have time to look around and then lowered me down onto the saddle, I mean his thighs, and then down to the ground, with Miss Adela helping him, I think, because it was more difficult to lower me down than to lift me up, I imagine, especially with the danger of the horse trampling me with its hooves, I think she patted affectionally my head in the process, which she often did, she appeared to like me, father said they'd take the horses to the stable and that he'd be soon home for lunch, and they trotted off along the pathway in the direction of the stables, Jan Amor doing again his fancy sideways dance, it was then I noticed it was still in the house, earlier, as I was playing in the bushes, I could hear through the open windows mother play the piano, something soft and gentle, I suspect something by Chopin, whom as I remember she adored, but then unexpectedly a stream of sharp rapid notes was heard again coming out of the house like a voice calling out angrily a stream of accusations in a dispute between two persons, I knew the composition well because mother would play it often, it was one of Bach's compositions, I believe the one from Book I of the Well-Tempered Clavier that sounds a little like the Russian song Two Guitars, both of which I was to get to know well when I grew up, but a white stallion? Sebastian? oh, yes, there was a beautiful white stallion the count owned, but nobody rode it, that is I don't think I ever saw anybody ride it, although, no, on second thought, I think I did, I did sometimes, occasionally, one of the grooms in the stable, a horse trainer or something, occasionally, infrequently but regularly did, to exercise it, him, the horse, I presume, I mean he, the stallion was used primarily as a stud lent out for a stud fee for impregnating mares, and otherwise was kept as a decoration, a toy, a beautiful toy to be admired, he spent most of his time in an enclosure, running around and showing off, neighing to other horses he'd see, wanting their company, he must have been an Arab purebred, with a small head on a curving muscular neck, like the head of a violin, an eighteenth-century Italian violin, an equine Stradivarius, with a shiny white body and a long white mane and tail, and black eyes and hoofs, small shiny hoofs like black porcelain cups his massive milk-white body was poured into, and would run around the enclosure when he saw someone come, to show off his grace and strength, his body rippling like a huge stream, a current of milk under pressure coming out of an orifice, jumping up and down and kicking up his heels, the head bent down as if he wanted to see a reflection of himself, to be pleased by the way he looked, I think that if they had a little pool of water, a spring or something in the enclosure, he would have stood there all the time admiring himself in it, his name was Narcissus, I presume because he was white but it fitted him especially well because of his being so in love with himself, but to me, when I say it, when I say his name, Narcissus, it sounds like, I mean, it means, Sebastian.

22

THERE'S A PERSON standing in the doorway, a man, strange, I don't think I've ever seen him before, although, no, wait, I think I have, he looks like Glenn Gould, yes, of course, it is, must be Glenn Gould, how wonderful! we've met before, on that hot muggy early June day, June tenth it was I think, yes, that's right, June tenth, when he came down to do, record his first version of the Goldberg Variations, flew in from Canada and took a taxi to the recording studio in midtown, brought along the icepick to hit the piano keys with, it was sticking out of his jacket pocket, jacket? no, pants pocket, the sharp point out, dangerous, but it would have been more dangerous the other way around, could have gone through the pocket lining and into his thigh, or even worse his erotic, genital region, stem of the penis or scrotum, scrotum? no, not scrotum, not likely, unless it, the scrotum was pushed up somehow, crazily, a real genital, scrotal contortionist, no, not likely, very much unlikely, stupid, enough, and of course I knew, know him socially too from later years, because of Roxy, not because I knew Roxy that well, or at all for that matter, but because of Marta, my editor and friend, friend of Roxy, they were close, well, good, decent, or at least just friends, acquaintances, and Roxy did an album with Glenn, she singing and he playing, playing the piano, of course, he's come to see me because my wife's at work and my son is indisposed, can't be here at the moment, he's busy, busy trying to get something for me or himself, my medicine and/or a drink, something with electrolytes for me perhaps or something for himself, an item of clothing, a book, or, say, a postage stamp, or he's having problems in his marriage or in his relationship, with his girlfriend, and is busy attending to them, attending to the problems, straightening them out, or simply because he's working, attending to his duties, doing what he's supposed to do in the course of a working day, he has to work to support himself and his family if he has one, of course, can't rely on us, his parents, or more precisely on his mother, who's the real bread winner in the family now, or at least he should be, should be working at his age, what is he? thirty, thirty-five, twenty-one? not sure, not if he's twenty-one, he doesn't necessarily have to work if he's twenty-one, should be going to school, studying, and in this case has the right to expect to be supported by his parents, and could, very likely is in school, college, finishing college, maybe, most likely not living with us, with his parents, but in another town, city, place, or even in another country, yes, of course, why haven't I thought of it, realized it before? would have spared myself a lot of grief, pain, worries, wouldn't have gone through all these variations of feeling bad, alone, abandoned, he's either working, or in school, or getting something for me or himself, or taking care of his personal problems, of which he must have plenty like every human being, every adult, and when he can, he will be here, standing in the doorway ready to assist me, be with me, give me physical and moral support, but in the meantime Glenn is here to keep me company, to speak to me about Bach, and William Byrd, and Orlando Gibbons, and Beethoven, and Mozart, and Schoenberg, and Webern, and Berg, and Strauss, Richard Strauss of course, not Johann, not Johann Strauss, not the Blue Danube and Vienna Woods Strauss but the one of *Vier letzte Lieder*, and the Piano Sonata in B-minor opus 5 he wrote when he was seventeen and patterned it on Mendelssohn, and the Violin Sonata in E-flat major opus 18 he wrote when he was twenty-four, and another composition in E-flat major, the Sonatina No. 2 he wrote when he was eighty-two or three, and all the other compositions which were not written for the piano but are transcribed, which deserve his attention and love, and about Bach, yes, of course, for Bach was the reason he, Glenn Gould became a pianist, he, that is Bach, was the most extraordinary musician that ever lived, the greatest nonconformist, greatest constructor, architect of sound, an artist of incredible linear imagination who in his works caried on a conversation with god and not with man as did Haydn and others, including his own sons, that came after him, he combined the northern, German and Dutch voice harmonies with the southern, Italian, instrumental ones, creating something lush and unique, never heard before, it wasn't until the twentieth century, when Schoenberg came along, that anything comparable was done in the field of harmony again, and about Orlando Gibbons too, who in spite of all of the above about Bach was his, Glenn's favorite composer, probably because of being more approachable, more on his level, someone who could be a friend, a buddy, whereas Bach was something else, amazing, daunting, a teacher, from whom you've learned all you know and can only admire, look up to, respect, but not be chums with, Byrd came along as a coeval, peer, accomplice in accomplishment, came riding in on the same record with Gibbons, and about

Mozart? to speak to me about Mozart? oh yes, with wit and relish moreover, accompanied by his esteemed and admired colleague with whom he couldn't disagree more, the mozartist, Sir Humphrey Price Davies, Mozart's late works, such as the Piano concerto in C-minor, are like an account executive's interoffice memos full of pet peeves that never want to end, an appalling collection of cliches and undistinguished harmonies, time-consuming scales and arpeggios, all easy to imitate, bad taste, I will add, impressive talent but bad taste, similar to that Spanish, Latin American writer, novelist, what's his name? Nodo? Nono? Dodo? Dono? Donatello? no, that's a sculptor, Donato? no, can't remember, the one who wrote that crazy book, The Crazy? no, not Crazy, something else, Stupid? maybe, yes, I think maybe Stupid, yes, The Stupid Bird of the Night, *El Estúpido pájaro de la noche* in Spanish, that's right, yes, with the man in it, the narrator, the mute one, who had eighty percent of his innards, organs removed by some crazy, evil doctor, Azaz? Azez? Aziz? Azoz? Azuz? something like that, don't remember, and lived on, what for? stupid! significant talent, no doubt, but bad taste, spoiled by Mary Shelly, that is, Frankenstein, and the comix, cartoons, whatever, not Juan Rulfo, not *Pedro Páramo* for sure, no, and Mozart?

what was Mozart spoiled by? certainly not by Frankenstein and comix, the public perhaps and need for money, easy money, an easy way to make a Gulden, or Thaler, or whatever the currency in Austria was called at the time, Thaler, I think, it was, yes, Thaler, I remember now, originally Joachimsthaler, from a village Joachimsthal in Bohemia where it was minted, the name meaning Joachim's Valley, *"Thal"* being "valley" in German, as it was spelled at the time, with an "h," now it's *"Tal,"* without, yes, Gulden was German, German and Dutch, nothing to do with Gould, Glenn Gould, of course, Gulden coming from "golden," in other words, a gold coin, "dollar," by the way, comes from "Thaler," so it was an easy way for Mozart to make a buck, a dollar, a thaler, by writing cheap, slick music, but he was spoiled by his own talent first and most of all, the ease with which scales and arpeggios, the space-fillers came to him, an easy way to make a living, and having nothing to say, was infantile, emotionally infantile, underdeveloped, something wrong with him hormonally too, thyroid? he was popeyed, I believe, his eyeballs bulged, struck out of their eye sockets, sometimes while playing the piano, he'd stop, get down on all fours, bark like a dog a few times, and go back to playing, composing, and he'd end letters to his wife Constanze with

Leck dein Ärschchen, Lick your little asshole, infantile, anal retentive, stuck in his terrible twos, his Requiem sounds in places like *Così fan tutte,* although his Symphony No. 40, the one in D-minor, it's good, almost like Bach but not quite, not quite, nothing and nobody quite is, I like it, the only thing of his I can stomach, like, something about that D-minor key, made even Mozart write something decent, non-trivial, and all those great Bach pieces in D-minor, amazing! something about it, about that key, the minor part, I guess, and four, the letter D? fourth letter of the alphabet? could be, the Japanese hate four, fear, abhor it, symbol of death, they say, don't know why, closed circle? to me it's great, closed circle is great, the task done, completed, absolved of responsibility, guilt, elegance, you've absolved yourself of your task most elegantly, Leonardo drew a perfect circle with one swoop of his arm to show how good he was, oh, but "death" starts with a "d" too, strange, never thought of that before, never noticed, but it's only in English, *Tod* in German, *mort* the morpheme *mort* for "dead" in many Indo-European languages, Romance *mortuus, mort, morto, morto, muerto* in Latin, French, Italian, Portuguese, Spanish, Slavic, *mertv, martv*, in Ukrainian and Polish, similar in other, but still, don't know, must dig more deeply into that, enough though for

179

now, back to the main topic, how are you Glenn? haven't seen you, heard from, heard you for a long time, how have you been? still looking good, good for your age, you're older than me, not much, a year and a half or so, I think, but still, you're older and look great, look like my son, are my son, one might say, amazing! you've brought me something? no? you didn't know what I need, can go out later and get it? yes, fine, something to drink, some juice or an electrolyte drink, to replace what I've lost, keep losing, sweating at night, you know those night sweats, those terrible night sweats when you wake up drenched to the skin with the bedlinen sticky as if someone had poured a bucket of water over you, and you feel yucky, reluctant to move, as if it made any difference, you moving, and what is it that you're holding in your hand? your chair, the rickety aluminum chair with the worn-out seat, without which you can't play because it's low and you have to have the keyboard right under your nose so that you see the keys real well and also so that you can sway easily as you play along in rhythm with the music because the piano benches are high and stiff and stubborn? Glenn, Glenn? where are you? he's gone, went downstairs to play for me, I hope, couldn't be otherwise, he couldn't have just left, gone away without saying anything, saying good-bye to me after

180

coming to see me on his own because I needed help, wouldn't make sense, play the variations, Glenn, the variations, the Goldberg Variations, you can play anything you want, anything by Bach, but I'd prefer if you'd play the Variations because that's what I need to hear right now, although at other times I'd take, listen to anything from you, even if not by Bach, but this time, please play the Goldberg Variations, the way you've played them, the way nobody has played them, either way, the way you played them the first time, that time in June, with your icepick, when we met, or the second time, years later, I think something like twenty-five years later, preferably the second time, the first one was a bit short, I'd like it to last longer, like the second time, so, please play it like that, there's a piano downstairs, Glenn, you can't miss it, you didn't bring your piano along, I don't think, at least you didn't bring it upstairs, didn't hold it in your hand like your chair, ha-ha, although with you anything is possible, any magic is possible, although you didn't do it this time, so, use that piano downstairs, Glenn, it used to belong to my mother, she used to play Bach on it in addition to other composers, Chopin most often, especially that piece from the Book I of the Well-Tempered Clavier that sounds like, sounds a little like the Russian Gypsy song Two Guitars, alright, I think he's heard me, I think I heard him shout back to me that he's heard me, that he saw the piano, which of course he couldn't have missed, but still replied that he had heard me, not necessary, but socially expected, polite, not an exchange of valuable information but a social convention, a way of satisfying expectation, not quite what's called a speech act, I think, like in Can you pass the salt? but close to it, a form of verbal behavior, alright, he'll play soon, I'll hear him play soon, soon? how soon? it should be, should have been seconds, a minute or two perhaps, but it's been longer than that, much longer, four, five, six minutes, they add up, time passes, I feel it flow by, feel it flow by me like a huge slow river, ten minutes, fifteen, no sound, still no sound coming from downstairs, in fact, stillness, I hear stillness, emptiness, the downstairs is empty, everything has been taken out of it, maybe my wife has moved out and taken everything with her, such things happen, especially with wives moving out, women have come into their own, with what the feminists have done, they have more rights, they, women complain about being disadvantaged, having unequal, lesser rights, bullshit! you try to be a man, especially a white man, but that's another story, a different kettle of fish, I'll not try frying it here, not in a kettle, not conducive, need a frying pan, don't have one right now, so it's best to put the matter aside at this time, the problem I'm faced with is different, more serious, silence downstairs, emptiness, wait, what piano was I talking about? mother's piano? I never had it, never had it in this house, it was lost, gone, years ago, gone if it ever existed, god knows if it did, objects are as ephemeral as deeds, but where is Glenn? is he gone? gone after being here minutes ago, after having come on his own to see me because I needed him? gone without saying a word to me, saying good-bye? Glenn! Glenn! Glenn! Orlando! Sebastian!

23

HAIL RANDOM, FULL of random, random is with…. no, no, not that, this, Our random, who art in random, hallowed be thy random, thy random come, thy random be done on random, as it is in random, give us this day our random random and forgive us our randoms, as we forgive our randomers, and lead us not into random, but deliver us from random, for thine is the random, and the random, and the random, for random, amen, it's snowing hard, and you have a doctor's appointment, and it's urgent, so you can't miss it, and how are you going to get there? and it's god who is behind it, making it hard, making it harder, making it very, very hard for you to do, and he's doing it on purpose, because he has something against you, and has always had something against you, since the day you were born, and even earlier, since you were conceived, no, even earlier than that, when you were planned, when the possibility of your being born, being there, arose, when your parents met, when they were born, when the concept of your being, the idea of

Yuriy Tarnawsky

someone like you being came into being in somebody's distant mind, and he has been rubbing it in ever since, watching you closely, following you closely, watching your every move to see when he could sting you, make it hard for you, make it harder for you, make it harder than at any other time, in any other situation, and it's like this for everyone or almost everyone, except for those who feel lucky, feel always on top, feel they have the world by the short hairs, feel god is always with them, god? with or against them? how many of them, how many of you are there? and I don't mean just people, but also animals, because they also may feel like that, have the right to feel like that, and not only animals, but plants too, why not? don't they have the right? who says they don't? how do we know? and microbes and viruses too, no, shouldn't mention microbes because they are animals, I think, and have been taken care of by what I just said, I mean thought, so also viruses, and anything else I haven't mentioned or don't know about, and not only here, here on earth, but everywhere, in the whole vast universe, on millions upon millions earths probably, and for trillions upon trillions of creatures, organisms perhaps on each, expecting, having a right to be treated fairly, exceptionally, with exceptional, with exceptionally favorite consideration, by whom? by that one miserable, unlucky, hapless creature, being, force, whatever, who on his/its own, of his/its own accord, volition decided to make, create them, us, fill the void with them, with us, first create the void, the space with nothing in it and then what's to go in and put it there? so by him/it? how? how could he/it possibly do that? how could he/it keep track of all of them, us? just think about it for a second, put yourself in his/its position, nonsense, sheer nonsense, anthropomorphic prejudice, blindness, a CPU, central processing unit, von Neuman's machine, architecture, a stored-program computer to handle all this? sheer nonsense, anthropomorphism, stupidity, lack of intelligence, but even here, on our earth we have counterexamples of that, of distributed intelligence, the octopus for instance, although I don't think that would help much, be less absurd, ridiculous, he/it would still have to do the tracking, evaluating, deciding, and it's that that is wrong, impossible, nothing, no decision point, no intelligence, pre-set, predetermined set of rules which enforce adherence to them, the legislative and judicial and executive power all in one, you follow the rule, you're rewarded, you break it, you're punished, penalized in a painful way or cashiered out of existence, you stick your hand in the fire, in a pot of boiling water, you're burned, your skin comes off, flesh is seared, you get an infection, whatever, you jump off a thousand foot-high cliff, the top of a ten story building, you're killed, that's it, that's all, no favors, no special treatments, he/it put together those couple, three, four, things, particles, bands of energy, phenomena, whatever you might call them and went to sleep, lay down to rest, it was hard work to create the universe with all the things, whatever, in it in six days, can you imagine? in only six days, how tired he/it must have been, exhausted, half- or even more- dead, those two-three, little things, particles, bands of energy, phenomena, whatever, and the random number I mean random event generator and *voici*, *voila,* presto! the whole system is in perfect working order, ticking like an expensive Swiss watch, clock, clockwork, silently purring along like an atomic clock, he/it is not dead though, I think, immortals don't die, but more than tired, exhausted, paralyzed, permanently paralyzed, a quadriplegic, unable to stir but able to see, appreciate the magnificence of the structure he/it created, watching with interest, admiration, immense satisfaction his/its accomplishment, himself/itself, a quadriplegic of cosmic proportions, dimensions, merged with nebulae, galaxies, stars, planets, tended, fed by comets and bees, washed by drops of dew and dried, fanned by monarch butterflies, his/its cheek, an itsy-bitsy, teeny-weeny part of his/its immense cheek lying in tall grass in some semi-abandoned backyard orchard in Eastern Europe, say, the outskirts of the city of Poltava, wherever, gently rotting away together with the plums that have fallen off the tree into the grass like it, and random? random number, I mean, random event generator? yes, it, the said, exactly, a perfect, reliable, one hundred percent sure executor, implementer of the established rules, established order, I, X, have gone through a zillion steps, events, deeds, some planned, others not, accidental, random you could say, which could but didn't have to have happened, and presto! once again, boom! one fine day I meet Y whom I instantly and madly fall in love with, marry, and who becomes my life-long loving, supporting partner, companion, for the rest of my long life, providence? god's will? hand? finger? love? no need to feel grateful, indebted, ignore it, shrug it off, randomness! random event generator! he/it didn't have anything to do with it, quadriplegic, rotting away slowly together with overripe plums in tall grass in a semi abandoned orchard in Eastern Europe, the outskirts of the city of Poltava, simple, done, no questions to be asked and answered, all due to the work of those super-super-miniature sub-sub-subatomic, diligent little workaholic ants-bands of energy, particles, events, whatever, he/it so cleverly put together, and the same thing with the snow, my doctor's appointment and the snowstorm, event, event, deed, event, event, I get sick, it's serious, I make an appointment to see my doctor, parallel to it event, event, event, culminating with snow, and presto! I have a dilemma, a near unsolvable problem and curse god, but it was again those super-super-miniature sub-sub-subatomic, diligent little workaholic ants-bands of energy, particles, events, whatever, he/it so cleverly put together, yeah, it's true, random doesn't mean accidental, unpredictable, causeless, for everything that is, is a result, and every result must have a cause, I am therefore I have a cause, but these series, series of events are so long, so complex that we can't possibly understand, fathom them, so that's why random, accidental, the result and cause rule incidentally is a proof that he/it isn't because what would have caused him/it? so you shouldn't use the word is with him/it but something else, but that's another matter, another kettle of fish, but I won't try frying it, them here without a skillet, amazing, simply amazing, don't understand why those die-hard bible ditto-heads, literalist believers, throw a tantrum, go ballistic, apoplectic when you suggest the world wasn't created in six days, light wasn't separated from darkness and water from earth, grass wasn't made to grow, fishes weren't plunked down in the sea, birds weren't shooed off to fly in the air, animals weren't set loose in the fields and woods, man, that is, Adam was not made from clay and Eve from his rib etc., but that things took a very, very long time to coalesce, and life evolved slowly, progressively, through the process of natural selection, and that we are related not only to apes but to cats and dogs, and to birds, and to fish, and ultimately to the smallest single-cell organisms such as amoeba, whatever, and all this because of those two-three-four bands of energy or particles, whatever, what brilliance, what incredible feat of science and engineering and perhaps even art, just think how magnificently green leaves of a tree contrast with the blue of the sky above them, and how breath-takingly the spectrum of colors at sunset towers above the dark horizon, and how blindingly the silver side of a fish flashes against the snow-white foam of a breaking wave! a super-super, many, many times super-super genius, the world itself and we in it are a proof, that is the world itself and we in it are the proof of his/its existence, even if he/it doesn't exist because there was nothing that could have caused him/it, but that's a small problem, a glitch in our language which doesn't have the word to describe his/its being which includes, means both is and isn't, because of our itsy-bitsy, teeny-weeny, yellow polka dot bikini feeble little brain.

24

GOING BACK TO snow for a minute, it's been a long and lonely winter, and we've had god knows how many snowstorms, ten? a dozen? more? almost certainly more, fifteen probably if not more, and it looks like it's not going to stop, like it'll go on forever, like it'll go on for still a long time, it's only the end of February and February and March are the worst months, the worst months for snow, most snow comes down during that time on average, so we can definitely expect more, and last night you cleared the snow off your two cars in the driveway and then shoveled the driveway itself after it had snowed on and off most of the day, it wasn't that much, three to four inches, and we've had nearly two feet once this winter and then over a foot last week, but still it was a pain in the ass, and this morning you get up and there's a miserable inch or so, maybe an inch and a half on the ground and on the damned cars, which is the worst place for it, for the snow to be on, much worse than on the ground, it takes roughly three times as much to clear off a car as to shovel the same amount of snow on the ground from the same-size area, an inch and a half isn't much but you can't leave it, first, you may need the car or both of them, and second, if it melts a little during the day and freezes at night, which is likely, it'll be much harder to clear it off in the future, when more snow comes down, especially on the cars, and besides, an inch and a half is just as slippery as four inches, or actually probably more so because it'll become slick sooner, and you don't want anyone walking up or down the driveway, like the postman or a delivery person, whoever, slip and fall and break his or her leg, and then you'll be sued, so you have to shovel the damned thing, the damned inch and a half, and you wake up in the morning and look out the window and see the damned miserable "near nothing" white thing, and your wife will be going to work soon, so she'll need the car, which means you have to clear the goddam thing off right away and shovel the driveway, and therefore you might as well do your car at the same time, and so you get dressed quickly, not having time to wash up properly and brush your teeth, and throw on some old clothes, and get the shovel and the broom for clearing off the cars, and as you start working on your wife's car, because it has to be ready as soon as she's ready to go away, and see what a chore it'll be to get the snow off with the broom, which you can visualize very vividly because of having done it not much more than twelve hours earlier, and you bite your teeth as you strain with what you're doing and say, You goddam sonofabitch, you vicious, evil bastard, an inch and a half, a miserable inch and a half! you couldn't have dumped it yesterday afternoon so that I'd have cleared it off with those three-four inches which would have made negligible difference? but no, you had to save it for this morning, and you probably don't have that much at your disposal right now, so you're saving some more for me for later today or for tomorrow morning, just like today, you goddam evil, puny little sonofabitch of a bastard! and you know he or it or whatever it is or isn't is paralyzed, and it's only those two-three-four bands of energy, particles, things, phenomena, whatever, and the random number, I mean the random event generator, randomness, a random event, but still you can't stop yourself from saying, You goddam evil, puny little sonofabitch of a bastard! because that's the only thing you can do, because it's the only recourse you have, because you're on the bottom of the totem pole, the pile, because you have nothing to say in these matters but to accept them, bite your teeth and bear it, because you know

195

that every thing, every effect, must have a cause, so you express your hatred at the cause, at what is making your life miserable, just this little concession, just this little easement, just this little chance, good Lord, give us just this little right to curse and hate you, you sonofabitch of a freak locked up there in your shabby one-room attic apartment so that no one sees you, you evil humpbacked dwarf with an over-acid stomach burning up your insides from an inexplicable hatred, stinking up with your sour breath the air around you, you who prevent people, men from having children, little boys to tell them stories about a boy and a girl who meet on moonlit, I mean, sunlit nights in the middle of an ocean with waters clear and magnifying as a magnifying glass, on the bottom of which there is a world with people in it, with fields and woods and roads and villages with red-roofed houses and churches with tall sharp spires, who then sail in a wind-blown ship that steers itself to a magic island that changes its shape where there lives a good fairy and four little gnomes and their friend, a brave little mushroom, where all sorts of marvelous things happen, such as you'll never see in real life, but that's nothing, that's very little compared to other things you do, such as ten-year old boys losing their mothers and fathers and home country practically on the

same day, and put them on trains to ride for days and days
with the purpose of ultimately being abandoned all alone in
the middle of nowhere in a hostile foreign country while
seeing the train going away from them trying at all cost to
disappear in the vanishing point on the horizon, boys who'd
done nothing to deserve it unless it be catching big fishes
with their hands and bludgeoning them to death with a stone
on the pebbled beach of the river they were caught in
because they thrash about too much and look frightening,
gasping greedily for water with their gills and mouth while
sucking in only thin air, and also drowning for someone, a
neighbor's newborn kittens by throwing them one by one off
a footbridge in the river while twirling some of them by their
tails and giving some of the others a painful squeeze on their
soft warm little stomachs that feel like fresh feces, and that's
also nothing or very little compared to creatures in Mexico
or wherever else it may be, probably of the female sex, girls
or young women, with deformed spines, no, deformed is not
the word, with spines practically gone, not there, so that as
they sit on the sidewalk their chins are practically on the
ground and look as if they were under the sidewalk with only
the upper chin above it, the big upper front teeth resting on
it, the huge complaining eyes staring complainingly, no,

questioningly ahead, seeing everything, the body a collection, an incomplete collection of bones gathered up hastily and shoved helter-skelter into a nearly black leather sack, a sack of human leather, skin, so these female creatures, girls or young women, that is, brown, nearly black leather sacks of incomplete collections of a person's bones gathered up hastily and shoved inside, while extending their hands for alms or not doing it, be it in Mexico or wherever else, see a haughty, handsome, athletic male angel, a white man, a *blanco*, stride by without touching the ground, uplifted, buoyed by the Adidas wings on his feet, without depositing even a centimo of *limosna*, alms, I mean glimmer of compassion in the pleading extended gaze, and then, barely one hundred feet or so farther, imagine, barely one hundred, no, fifty, barely fifty feet farther on, after turning left onto the street that together with the other three forms a little square, in front of the door leading to a restaurant, meets a girl, a beautiful tall, slender, Texas-sky blue-eyed girl and they kiss, they stand and kiss, without embracing but standing close together and kissing on and on and on, to rub it in, to make sure the brown, near-black leather sack of an incomplete collection of a person's bones sees it, absorbs every drop, molecule of it, gets as much pain as possible out of it, you evil humpbacked dwarf with an over-acid stomach burning up your insides from an inexplicable hatred, stinking up with your sour breath the air around you, the whole world! ugggggggggggggggggggggggggggggggggggggggggggggggggggggggh! you bastard!

25

THERE'S A MAN standing in the doorway, he seems familiar but I can't place where I know him from, can't think of his name, looks a little bit like me when I was young, but of course it's not me, couldn't be, I'm here in bed, so I couldn't be in the doorway at the same time unless I were one of those entangled subatomic, quantum particles or whatever they are called which can be in two different places at the same time, unless I am a subatomic quantum particle, which I am not, not yet anyway, but one day perhaps I will be, like the rest of us, anyway, it's not me, so who can it possibly be? my god, yes, of course, it's Marlon Brando, the way he looked in A Streetcar Named Desire, in the film, and in his other films, early films, Viva Zapata, and The Wild Bunch, no I think it was called The Wild One, yes it was The Wild One, with him on a motorbike leading a bunch of thugs like him, and maybe even On the Waterfront, him being, playing Terry Malloy, in which he could have been a contender, but no, he was older and heavier then and I didn't look like that when I looked like him, I used to see him when I came into the city on Saturdays, late at night, when he'd come out of the acting school on Lafayette Street, I think Actors Studio it was called, yes, Actors Studio, run by Lee Strasberg and Stella Adler and later Elia Kazan, no, not Lee Strasberg, yes, Lee Strasberg, although Brando didn't like him and said he didn't learn anything from him except from Stella Adler and later from Elia Kazan, but Strasberg did run the studio, anyway, it's across the street from what's now The Public Theater, although, no, I think it's on the same side a little ways south, downtown, yes, on the same side a little ways downtown, of course, because uptown, north, is Astor Place, or actually a parking lot, I think, at least there was one at the time, now there's a big glass building probably, and then Astor Place, anyway, when I'd come to see my friends, my drinking buddies at the Orchidia on Second Ave and Nineth Street, the Italian place ran, owned by, Paul, Paulo, we called him, although he seemed to be uncomfortable with it, with the name, with Paolo, tried to hide he was Italian, was ashamed, I guess, ashamed, afraid of being called a Wop, although I don't know why anyone would be ashamed of being Italian, Dante, and Michelangelo, and Leonardo, and Botticelli, and Farinelli, and Torricelli, and Modigliani, and Magnani, and Mastroianni, and Bernini, and Bellini, and Puccini, and Albinoni, and Busoni, and Marconi, and Fibonacci, and Fermi, and Verdi, and, and, and no end to the Ellis, and the Anis/Inis/Onis, and the Is in general, and who, that is, Paul/Paulo was robbed of it, robbed of the restaurant after he dropped his wife, his wife Marina, I think that's what she was called, dropped his wife Marina for a young Italian chick, whom he transferred the ownership to so as not to lose the place, lose part of it in the divorce, and then she, the chick left him and sold it behind his back, poor Paolo, in the end was left with nothing, no wife, no restaurant, no chick, worked as a waiter after that, I heard, anyway, I'd see my friends at other places too, of course, although Orchidia most of the time, and we'd get drunk and wander around the area late at night, almost empty at the time, and Brando would come out of the studio, the narrow doorway, hair flying, eyes ablaze after the class, striding with others excited like him, gesticulating, while moving down the empty wide, nearly dark sidewalk, and also, I'd see him also sometimes as I'd walk from the subway station to the restaurant, to the Orchidia, no, god, what am I saying? he was no longer there when I was meeting my friends, when I would come into the city on Saturdays, he was in Hollywood

203

already, had made The Streetcar which I saw and loved, and
Zapata, and The Wild One, and Julius Caesar, I think, yes,
that too, and maybe even On the Waterfront, yes, of course,
that too because I didn't even graduate from college yet
when it was made, which was a couple of years later, so I
didn't see him then, not walking from the subway station and
not after the restaurant, didn't see him ever, at all, just
imagined seeing him after seeing all those movies of his and
imagining, imagining myself looking like him, what man my
age wouldn't have? Tarzan! they'd call out to me when I was
on the beach or even elsewhere, like at a fair or something,
if I wore a T-shirt, and I'd stop and show off, flexing my
biceps and winking, I mean twitching my pecs, my face
serious, god, how stupid you are when you're young! and,
Hey you, Brando! Marlon! and I'd glance at them from the
corner of my eye, from under the eyebrows, the puffy
eyelids, the corner, the same corner of my mouth as the eye
swollen with a smile, with his smile, as if from a passionate
bite in a passionate kiss with a passionate girl, my straight
nose curved down as much as possible, as much as my
facial muscles would permit to resemble his, Brando's, once,
I think I was called Brando, but Tarzan many, well, a few
times, and also Atlas, Atlas more than Tarzan, Tarzan was

largely forgotten by then, stupid! how stupid, vain I was, believing that stuff, maybe if they'd called out to me, Hey you, Mickey Rooney! I would have believed that too, no way, never, I did sort of look like him at the time, like Brando, trying with all my might to, dressing, and combing my hair, and looking up from under my eyebrows, and smiling, and having that full, smooth face rather than a bony, chiseled one of a mature he-man, and being of the same build and height as he, or actually a bit taller, a quarter or half an inch or so taller, I think, so I couldn't have looked like Mickey Rooney, that undersized underaged wonder with his ugly, freckled Irish face, and was always thinking girls should chase me, although looks don't always help you, or hurt you for that matter, hurt a man, it's different for girls, there are other things that may count more, look at Rooney, he married Ava Gardner, that is, Ava Gardner married him, he, an undersized little freckle-faced pipsqueak of an Irishman and she a dark beauty, one of the most beautiful women in Hollywood at the time, perhaps the most beautiful ever, what a mismatch, but it did happen, well, some girls did chase me, although not all, especially not the ones I chased, that is I wanted, I never chased anyone, any girl, but drunk, with a bunch of my drinking buddies, in some bar, not in Orchidia,

we were never that drunk there, eating, and, drinking, and
chatting, chatting   about art, and existence and essence,
and essence and existence, and existence and essence, so
in some bar after Orchidia, when really drunk, with the
desperation in me having risen up to the surface like the
sharp end of a stick out of a swamp, I'd remember that
telephone number some barman once gave me, would leave
the others at the table, walk up to the payphone on the wall,
and call it, call the number, Can I speak to Dominick, the
television repairman? he was never there, not a single time
after dozens of calls over, in the course of maybe two years,
never there, He's not in right now. Call back in an hour, once
or twice I called back in an hour but got the same spiel, He's
not in right now. Call back in an hour, I don't know what it
was, a scam or a joke? I don't think a scam, there was no
profit in it for anyone, and no joke either, what for? he was
supposed to fix you up with a girl, a prostitute, and I tried it
for almost or actually more than two years, some Marlon
Brando! back to the subway for a ride back home, but prior
to that the obligatory photo session in an automat, dozens
and dozens of them, poses like Rudolph Valentino, Robert
Taylor, Stewart Granger, Tyrone Power, but mostly Marlon
Brando, glancing from the corner of my eye, from under the

eyebrows, the puffy eyelids, the corner of the mouth swollen with a smile as if from a bite in a passionate kiss with a girl grown wild from kissing, the straight nose curved down as much as my facial muscles would permit to resemble his, but Rooney? could someone have thought I looked like Mickey Rooney? aside for the height, why not? a pair of eyes, a pair of ears, one nose, an ass, sure, everyone looks like everyone else, let me see better, crane my neck, yes, it's him, Hi, Marlon, how are you? I mean where have you been for so long? Did you get it, get what you needed? And the medicine, the electrolyte drink for me? What are you saying? you're mumbling, mashing up the words like you always did, they didn't teach you to enunciate clearly in that Actors Studio, Stella Adler, Elia Kazan, and Lee Strasberg? sure they did, you just didn't want to do it on the screen, not usually, not for the characters you played, like Stanley Kowalski, or Terry Malloy, or the character from The Wild One, Johnny, what was it? Johnny Starker? no, Stabler? no, St, Str, Strabler, yes, Johnny Strabler, I think, it wasn't proper, right, they didn't speak like actors do on the stage, you did it properly, clearly, in Julius Caesar, playing Mark Antony, when it was appropriate, but not in the other roles, films, always your way, appropriate, when they said, pretend you're a chicken and an atom bomb is about to fall on your head, all the other students ran around like crazy cackling and trying to hide but you sat still, hatching your eggs, I'm a chicken, What does a chicken know about the atom bomb? you said, and you were right, as always, right, hair flying, eyes ablaze as he stepped out of that narrow door of Actors Studio, striding with others excited like him, gesticulating while moving down the wide sidewalk of Lafayette street? no way, no way, José, not him, he, who sat quietly hatching his eggs while others ran around like chickens with their heads chopped off because an atom bomb was falling on their heads, not knowing what to do, never excited, perhaps mad sometimes, yes, like in A Streetcar, but never excited, like that cool and cocky Johnny Strabler terrorizing the little town he and his gang invaded in The Wild One or calm and pensive like Terry Malloy trying to explain himself to his brother in On the Waterfront, you didn't come to bring me anything? no, of course not, how stupid of me, to scream, yes, you've come to scream, so scream for me Marlon, scream as you have screamed and as nobody else has ever screamed or ever will, Steeeeellaaaaan! Steeeeellaaaaan! Steeeeellaaaaan!

26

OK, ALRIGHT, DADDY and Sebastian will have quality time together this morning, just the two of us guys, two guys, man bonding, man and boy bonding, father and son bonding, they speak a lot about mother and daughter, mother and daughter bonding, but we will have father and son bonding, alright? mommy? mommy gone? not coming back? god no, why do you say that? mommy's at work, working to support us, to bring in more money because daddy's pension isn't enough, isn't as big as it used to be, has shrunk a lot lately, so mommy goes to work so that we, mommy, daddy, and you have enough, live better, live well, she'll call at lunchtime as always and talk to us on the phone, and will be home for supper, to fix it, or to help us, to help you and me fix it and have it together, the three of us, yes, don't worry, mommy hasn't gone away, hasn't left us, we're together, we're a family, we'll always be a family, will always be together, the three of us, don't worry, but this morning you and me, you and daddy will have quality time together, guys' time, men's time, man and boy, father and son together, bonding, alright? alright, we'll go running, like daddy has always done, like he's been doing it for many years, alright? you want to do it? great, alright, oh, the lace on this shoe is loose, untied, let me fix it, wait, stay still, now good? feels good? not loose? no? OK, you like your shoes? they're nice? like mine? yes, except smaller, of course, now let's stretch, OK, lean against the wall like this and stick one of your feet out, this foot out, like that, yes, press down and hold it, yes, OK, hold it, hold it, and feel it stretch in the back, the Achilles' tendon? you do? good, OK, hold, hold, now the other one, press down and hold, hold, feel it stretch? good, OK, hold, hold, now bend down and touch your toes, bend down, down, more, more, keep your leg straight, straight, yes, keep on bending, keep; on bending, and now touch your toes with your fingers, a little more, yes, OK, and now with your palms, the ground with your palms, with the palms of your hands, touch the ground with the palms of your hands, but keep the legs straight, you can't? it's alright, it'll do, you have to stretch a lot before you can do it with your palms, and one day you'll be able to do it., but it's alright now, you don't need it, you're still small, you'll need it when you get older and run a lot, but you have to stretch before each run and then afterwards, the muscles get a workout during the run and contract, shrink, so you have to stretch them, otherwise you'll get a backache and ultimately won't be able to run, so you have to do it often, all the time, to stay loose, limber, limber and strong, OK, now let me do it, yes! yes! yes! wow! that feels good, you'll remember how I did it? yes? OK, try to do it next time like that, OK? fine, now we're ready, no, wait, I have to put the key in the sock, it may fall out of the pocket when we run but when you hide it in the sock, it's safe, we need it, need it to get back inside, you wouldn't want to have to stay outside and not be able to get in, would you? mommy? mommy's key? yes, we could use mommy's key, but we'd have to wait till supper, for many hours, six, seven, when she gets back, and not be able to go inside and have a drink, and lunch, and go to the bathroom, and wash up, too long, yes, OK, now we run, you beside me, yes, close to the curb, we turn right here, yes, and then right again, right, right, yes, and up the hill, hard? out of breath? no,? no, you're young and it takes a lot to make you run out of breath, a lot of running, a little, a little out of breath, OK, we'll walk now, walk a little to catch our breath, you want me to carry you? no? good! never give up, never let anyone carry you or stop, walk if you have to but never stop, never give up on anything in life, finish, you

always must finish whatever you've started, OK? yes? good!
OK, we're on   top now, we can jog, run again, feel the soft
earth, path under your feet now? you do?   good, it feels
good, doesn't it? yes, it's always advisable to run on soft
ground, good for your feet, legs, knees and other joints, the
spine, doesn't hurt them like concrete and asphalt does,
remember how it felt when we ran up the hill?   was it hard?
yes? now it isn't, it's soft, nice and pleasant, comfy, like being
tucked in under warm covers in bed, like mommy or daddy
do for you, yes? good, mother earth always takes care of us
if we let it, yes, it's our mother, mother of us all, daddy?
daddy of us all? I guess it's god, what people call god, the
force, the energy that's behind all this, behind the world and
us, behind us and mother earth, see the empty space there
on the right, below? water? yes, it's a lake, the lake we were
at when you ate the worm, remember? no? yes? you do?
OK, I've been telling you about it, remember, with the swans,
the baby swans, swanlings? yes, with the swanlings, the
baby swans, we're going there, will run along it, OK, how's
the running now? you're tired? out of breath? no? good, you
want to walk? walk a little? OK, you've got to be careful here
running, there are rocks and tree roots on the path, you may
catch your toe on them and fall down, hurt yourself,

remember when we went fierce rabbit hunting at home? what I told you? yes? yeah, you can go flying and hurt yourself, hurt yourself badly, I can't carry you on my shoulders here because if I fall down you'd really go flying along the path, even farther than me, real far, yeah, and tree trunks and big rocks, running into them? when the path curves? oh, yes! very dangerous, there, look, there's a big rock, cliff, over there, where the path curves, you'd really hurt yourself if you ran into it, like a door? a closed door? no? like an open door? oh, solid air? stone air? yes, you're right, rocks are like spaces filed with stone rather than air and if you enter them you enter a stone world, very true, and you don't want to enter a stone world, it'd be hard to live there, hard to breathe, you'd choke, your lungs would fill up with stone, very difficult, it's very difficult to breathe, live inside a stone, no, we don't want to run into that rock, enter it, or any other, alright, there are steps here, so you have to go down them carefully so as not to fall, to go flying down them head over heels, yes, very dangerous, even more than catching your foot on a rock or a root on the path, OK, we can jog now, run a little, you're OK? good, but be careful, nice, the path is nice and soft here and straight, OK, out of breath? you ran fast, too fast, you get out of breath then and can't run afterwards, must walk or jog slowly, yes, you have to be careful, pace yourself, so that you don't run out of breath, run into oxygen deficit, debt, but that you can continue running as long as you have to, look there's a brook there, the one I told you about, with the water so beautiful, remember? yes, see the water? beautiful? really beautiful, it can flow like tears, it can flow where tears flow from, it can flow where tears flow to, it covers the earth like grass, it can kill like a sword, it can kill like an atom bomb, it can be compared to anything, careful now, we're going down some steps again, bigger, longer steps, they curve too, careful, it's hard to walk here let alone run, be careful, don't fall down, OK, there's the lake there we saw from higher up, remember, yes, we'll be running along it on the way back home, will turn right, OK, careful, we have to cross the brook again, the same brook as the one above, it's the same, except it's more turbulent here, the water's all roiled up after coming down the steep long hill, and there's no bridge here, no footbridge here as there was up there, made from big flat sones, yes, we have to ford it, get across it by jumping over rocks, I mean, from rock to rock, careful, not beautiful? the water's not beautiful? roiled up? beautiful, still beautiful, it can kill like an atom bomb but it's still beautiful, it's transparent but it's there, it exists, it is and it isn't, that's beautiful, isn't it? yes, you remember? yes? OK, now up the bank a little, the slope, here, give me your hand, alright, it's still a bit rocky here, so we won't run, a little farther on, it's flat and soft underfoot there, see the lake now? white, yes, looks like the sky, reflects the sky, that's why, like a mirror, yes, where we were last year, no, the year before, I think, yes the year before last year, at the other side, where you ate that earthworm, ugggh, yuck, yes, ugggh, yuck, you wouldn't, won't do it again, no, of course not, and over there is where the two swans, the couple used to come each spring and have their babies, now no more, no swans anywhere, pollution and stress, yes, pesticides and houses popping up everywhere, green space disappearing, yes, oh, the little ones I told you about were so beautiful, gray, with shiny black beaks like the finest Chinese lacquer, and they would swim in the wake after their mother down the lake, so beautiful, now no more, swans and other birds not having babies any more, eggs not hatching, eggs not being laid, pollution, yes, pesticides and stress, yes, creatures are dying out, OK, enough, we can run now, feel OK? alright, soft underfoot, right? feels good, like a carpet, like the carpet in the gym we went to once? yes, you didn't like it there? no, me either, smelled bad, strange, too many people, too much equipment, outside's better, here it's better, smells nice and no people, no machines, just trees and brooks, trees and a brook and a lake , OK, feel strong? want to do fartlek, intervals? speed training? run fast for a little distance and then slowly, OK, let's try now, I'll show you first and then you try, OK? stay here, I'll be back, whew! that was good! OK, you do it now, but don't turn around, just run fast a little and then slow down, go on, you run and I'll catch up with you, I'll run fast too and slow down, run! run! whew! that feels good! let's jog now a little and then do the speed workout again, like it? yes? OK, daddy? daddy fast? yeah, I used to be pretty fast, had a strong kick, could overtake anyone at the end, but not so great at long distance, good, but not great, champion? no, I wasn't a champion, but maybe could have been, could have been a contender, I told you about how one spring I couldn't run in the big marathon because I'd gotten sick earlier and couldn't train, so on the marathon day I ran alone in the park four hundred meters and was just a few seconds off the world record for seniors, people over forty, maybe like five, six, or seven, that's not that great but I ran alone, without any prior training, and having been sick a few weeks before, so I probably could have broken that record in competition, on a track, having prepared myself properly beforehand and perhaps could have done it too for the real world record when I was young, your grandfather, my dad? yes, he was very fast too, he won the final four hundred meter run in the military officer school, when he was graduating, with two hundred men competing, first out of two hundred! that's pretty good, it's inborn, something you're born with, your genes, I look like him, so I got it from him, and you too, you should be fast too, have a good kick, you look like me, a lot like me, like me and my dad, your grandfather, so you should be a good four hundred meter runner, you want to? yes? great, we will train together, OK, we'll run just a little more, to the end of the lake, to cool off, you should always do that, to let your muscles relax and not cramp up, because you'd have a backache afterwards? yes, exactly, see the little park there, where you ate that worm? OK, but we won't go there today, some other time, for lunch, maybe next week, fine, now we just walk, go back up this steep slope to where we came into the woods from the street and then turn left onto the path leading out, then down the path to the street, and then down the street home.

27

THE SEA, YES, you've seen it a few times when you were little, but you don't remember it, you were too small, we weren't able to come the last few years because of mommy's working, her being busy all the time, too busy, even on weekends, and I didn't want to bring you myself because you were too little, but now you're big, so we can come when mommy's working but will be back before she comes home and we'll help her fix supper or maybe will cook supper ourselves, OK? yes? would you like that? OK? good, that's what we'll do, the sea, it's like the one in the story I've been telling you about Flamino and Flamina, when they meet at night, she in the little silver boat and he in the big beautiful sail ship with huge sails like giant white swans, no, it's not transparent like that, not like a magnifying glass over land where you can see forests, and fields, and rivers, and roads, and towns, and villages, and buildings and people in them underneath, no, that was, that is an enchanted, magic, special sea, you can see, go to at night in a fairytale, and

Yuriy Tarnawsky

this one is a regular, everyday sea, but it's beautiful too, maybe even more beautiful than the other one, you can go to it any time, every day, can see it, touch it, get inside it and taste it, you like it? yes? yes, of course, it's like a huge blue tank advancing toward the land, us, see how high it rises on the horizon way over there? no? not a tank, too wide? yes, you're right, it is too wide, but if you look just at part of it, then it's narrow and looks like a giant blue tank ready to advance, no? a book? like a giant closed blue book? yes, you're right, it is like a giant closed blue book, when you open it there're all sorts of wonderful things written in it, not in words, in letters, A, E, W, X, Z I've been telling you about, teaching you, but in things, written in things, like fishes, all sorts of fishes, small, and big, and giant, sharks and swordfish, and other sea creatures like whales, and dolphins, and manatees, and squid, and octopuses, remember the one you saw in the TV program, Heidi, I think, it was called, yes, Heidi, probably because it liked to hide, she was a pet, and liked people and could recognize them, and missed them when they weren't around, yes, Heidi, who especially liked the little girl, the daughter of the scientist who studied her, yes, what was her name? I don't remember, do you? no? that's fine, maybe they didn't tell the girl's name in the

220

program although they probably did, they almost definitely did, it doesn't matter, so all sorts of living creatures and things, objects, like rocks, and sand, and sunken boats, old boats, boats made of wood, galleons they're called, full of treasure, and iron ones like luxury ocean liners, and oil tankers, and military boats, troop carriers, and submarines, German submarines, and so on, it's also like a computer, isn't it, a liquid supercomputer doing millions of operations per a tiny fraction of a second, computer? what daddy spends much of his time at, what happens inside it, the goings on, the circuits, electronics working busily all the time, it's too complicated for you to explain, too boring, you'll learn about it in due time, will have your fill of it, too much, don't worry, it's like millions and millions of little fingers under the water counting and signaling, and pointing, whatever, and getting all sorts of calculations done, herding numbers like giant flocks of sheep in a file, into a thin little line, in the right direction, through a tiny little gate, yes, come on, we'll make ourselves comfortable over there, in the lee of the dune, dune? dunes? mounds of sand, they're mounds of sand, see them stretching way in the distance like waves, like waves of sand? waves? on the water? they are waves not dunes, they're called waves, and dunes? they are waves of sand?

yes, that's what they are except we call them dunes, they don't move like the waves in the sea, they sit still, except no, wrong, they do move but very, very slowly, move with the wind, especially in the desert, in vast open spaces filled with sand, oceans of sand, they move very, very slowly but they do move, see the green grass on top of some of the dunes, very thin, you can barely see it, it's like the spray on top of the waves, the waves in the sea, see it? no? yes? yes, a little, right, the grass is like the spray of water on the crests of the sea waves, nice? yes, right, nice, it's like poetry, the dunes are like poets creating metaphors, visual, physical metaphors, comparing themselves to sea waves and sea waves to them, beautiful, the world is beautiful, full of poetry except you have to be a poet to see it, it's great, it's great to be a poet and see beauty constantly, all around you, except you feel pain too, there's a lot of pain in the world too mixed in with beauty and you feel the pain when you see the beauty, see the beauty through the pain and pain through the beauty, you're better off not being a poet, don't see or feel much, just yourself, your body and things around it, don't be a poet, be a mathematician, physicist, whatever, a sportsman, athlete, yes, a sportsman best, you're active all the time, healthy, in touch with yourself, your body, and you make a lot of money, good money if you're a good athlete, you're best being a sportsman, Sebastian, we'll run together more and you'll be a runner, make lots of money running and not thinking about life, just putting one foot before the other one, right-left, right-left like what you do in running a marathon, your mind's shut off and all you are is a machine, a device, an organism that puts one of its feet before the other one, over and over, over and over, like a runner in a marathon, and in life too, you put one day before the other one, or maybe it's the other way around in life, one day behind the other one, the old one behind the new one, yes, the old one behind the new one in life it is, like your feet the other way around in a marathon, yes,   OK, so be a marathoner, marathoners make a lot of money, the champions, when you win an important marathon you make a huge sum of money and sometimes get a new car too, it's great, not like other sports where you have contact with other players and may get hurt, it's great, you just shut off your mind and put one foot in front of the other one, but I don't know if you'd be a great marathoner, I wasn't because I was too big, too heavy, heavy-boned, you need light bones to be a great marathoner, and you look like me, so you may be a good sprinter or four hundred meter runner but not a marathoner, like my father, your grandfather was and I probably could have been as I told you before, remember? yes?, OK, I don't think these kind of athletes, the runners who don't run marathons, make as much money as marathoners do but we will see, you should be what you want to be, and you will be what you will be, a runner like me probably, and a poet too, you saw a closed book in the sea, so there's a poet in you, and it's not all bad, it's not bad to see beauty everywhere and all the time, some people, millionaires, billionaires, would give a lot of money to see it, and you will do it for free, free! so it's not all bad, what does a little or a lot of pain matter when you see a whole lot of beauty, mountains, oceans of beauty, but that's enough, let's go for a swim, in the water, here, let's arrange our things here nicely, like that, yes, the bag, the towels, the cooler here, yes, and take our clothes off, fold them neatly, like that, yes, and put them neatly here before we go in the water, it's safe here, there're few people around, and we'll see from the water if anyone comes close to our things, oh, wait, I have to put some suntan lotion on you and myself, wait, wait, here we are, stand still, I have to put it all over you, yes, and now myself, wait, wait, we have to do it so as not to get sunburned, remember how mommy got sunburned by staying too long in the sun? how red she got and swollen? yes, OK, we're done, we can go in now, let's run, run, run, run, whew! ha-ha-ha! Here, grab my hand, whew! the waves are strong, stubborn, unpleasant, they don't want to let you come into the water, they say, no! no! no! stay out! stay out! it's our place, stay out! yes, exactly, like those bad kids in the kindergarten, like that nasty little girl that used to push you and make you fall down all the time? yes, her mother was surprised at her, said she didn't behave like that at home, see, you're a poet already, that's great, it's better to be a poet than not, and a runner too, this way you have the best of two worlds, that's what daddy did, do you want to do that too? yes? great! you make daddy very happy, you're happy too? great! OK, let's go in deeper, I'll hold you in my arms, here, yes, feel how the water carries us, rocks us up and down like the branch of a tree on which we're sitting, going up and down, up and down, nice, nice, right? yes, beautiful, like that rocking horse in the park, yes, you're growing as a poet right now, before my eyes, wonderful, we're having a wonderful time, wonderful, quality time together, just the two of us, you and me, mommy told us to have a good time, to have quality time together, some guys' time, father and son time, go to the beach, yes, she's a very good mother, she loves us both and wants us to love each other, and to love her too? yes, of course, and we do, right? yes, very, very much, she goes to work every day to help us live better, and does things at home too, many, most of things, although we do some too, right? yes, some cleaning up, vacuuming, and dusting, and doing the dishes, and cooking, are you getting hungry? soon? in seven minutes? good in seven minutes we'll go out and dry ourselves and have lunch, tuna fish sandwiches, yes, there are four of them, and you will have how many? two? there? no, that's too much, you can't eat that much, you think you will but you won't be able to, they're big, they're with that bread I baked last night, the fluffy slightly sweet one you like, from white flour and oatmeal, but if you finish two and are still hungry, you can have part of the third one, part of what we were going to share later before heading home, OK? OK, and milk, you'll have your milk and I my beer, my Mexican beer, Modelo, yes, to look like a model, male model, well, at least I'll try, it's hard at my age to look anything other than myself, OK, and we'll stay here for a couple of hours more, go in the water a couple of times, and then clean off, dry off, and head home to beat the traffic, it'll take us over an hour to get home, so we have to make sure we'll be home in time to make supper for mommy and us, OK? what do

you think we should have? fish? yes? pink fish? you mean
the red fish you like? red snapper? good, OK, we'll stop off
at the seafood store and pick up a nice plump red snapper
and grill it outside for supper as we always do, there's still a
lot of the bread left, so we'll have it with the fish and with
salad, some green salad with onion and garlic, and oil and
vinegar, OK? and ice cream? you'll have ice cream for
dessert? yes, of course, and mommy probably too, but not
daddy, not if he wants to look like a male model, what ice
cream do you want? manila, manila ice cream? yes? good,
you'll have manila ice cream, with apple sauce? sure, you
can have it with apple sauce, anything else? and a banana?
a banana then it'll be, manila ice cream with apple sauce and
a banana, that's all? two bananas? two bananas? no!
Sebastian, stop it! no! you can't have a second banana, it's
too much, you'll throw it away, what? it's a joke? just one?
you want just one? you were joking? you're terrible,
Sebastian, you're really something! sometimes you're really
something! I don't know what I'm going to do with you or
would do without you, are the seven minutes up yet? yes,
good, we're going out, the beach? it's like cobwebs, like
cobwebs in the distance in both directions? you're right, the
beach, the world is like cobwebs hanging in the corner way

Yuriy Tarnawsky

off in the distance, barely there, I seem to be a bad
housekeeper, don't clean our place well, for you must have
seen lots of cobwebs in the house, I must shape up, clean
better, get those cobwebs up in the corners with the vacuum
cleaner, you're getting more and more of a poet by the
minute, by the time we get home you'll be better than your
father, what? a chest of drawers? the sea's like a big chest
of drawers? a chest of drawers full of things? gee, yes,
you're right, it's like a huge chest of drawers painted blue,
with the waves like drawers you can pull out and all those
things, fishes, and dolphins, and octopuses, and squid,
whatever, and sunken ocean liners, and galleons, and
German submarines inside them, yes, boy! you're better
already, you're a better poet than your father is already, no
need to go home.

28

THERE'S A BOY standing in the doorway, a little boy, maybe four or five, who could it be? I don't know any boys that age, and how could he have gotten into the house anyway? it's strange, is he someone else? am I someone else? Sebastian, how are you? where have you been so long? did you get the things for me? for yourself? you know, the prescription medicine, the electrolyte drink, drinks, the things you need? what was it? balloons? a balloon? yes, you did, you're holding it in your hand, on a string, it rises, I mean it's floating up in the air, tilting this way and that like a head trying to get a better look at something, at me? why? is there something wrong with me? does it want to do something to me? strike me like a venomous cobra to hurt me, to kill me? Sebastian, it's red! it's red, Sebastian! it wants blood, it's gorged with blood, smeared with blood, your blood, it'll take you away, Sebastian, like it did that little boy Pascal in the Lamorisse film, the 1956 Albert Lamorisse film Le Balon rouge, The Red Balloon, you'll die like him, like his son Pascal in the film, like he himself in the helicopter crash filming his last film The Wind? The Lonely Wind? no, The Wind of Others, I mean The Wind of Lovers, yes, the Wind of Lovers, the helicopter, the evil helicopter picked him up in its strong sharp claws and dropped him, dropped him onto the hard, rocky soil of Iran, onto the parched soil of Iran strewn with sharp rocks so that he'd be smashed to pieces, I mean, so that he'd be smashed to a messy, bloody pulp, like the evil red balloon that picked up his son Pascal and lifted him way up into the sky and dropped him onto the hard sidewalks of Paris, onto the shap-peaked Parisian house roofs, onto the sharp spire of the Sainte Chapelle, the Notre Dame, the Eifel Tower, no, I'm getting confused again, it's strange how I remember all these names and numbers and all but don't remember events, facts of life, my life, it means something of course, something important, although I don't know what, it bothers me, but what can I do? life is, I mean, I am what I am and it won't change, that's all, anyway, no, the balloon didn't drop the boy but merely carried him away never to be seen again, which for all practical purposes is the same, and it wasn't just the red balloon, but a bunch of others, a whole bunch of others, the red balloon's friends, who came to help it, help the balloon, the red balloon, carry the boy away, and actually, I think the red balloon was no longer there, it expired, I mean it was deflated, it was punctured by some boys who shot at it with slingshots, and then the friends of the red balloon, a whole bunch of balloons of various colors came and carried the boy away never to be seen again just as the eagle that Zeus turned into carried the beautiful boy Ganymede to Olympus, which for all practical purposes was as good as, I mean as bad as killing him, give it to me, Sebastian! come here and give it to me! it'll carry you away, it'll take you away and we'll never see each other! come! he laughs, turns around, and runs down the hallway, I jump out of bed and chase after him, he giggles as he runs, turning his head back from time to time to look at me with his smiling eyes, his bare feed making loud thud, thud, thud sounds on the bare wooden floor, the balloon on the string swinging from side to side and bobbing up and down, nearly black in the unlit space like a giant, impish, buoyant blood clot, I chase after him, seeing him turn left at the end of the hallway, thankfully get safely past the empty space of the staircase going down on the left, and charge through the door into the little room flooded with daylight, I'm almost on his heels as I pass through the door, and as the balloon starts lifting him up, I lunge, grab him around his waist and

231

bring him down together with myself onto the hard bare hardwood floor, I turn onto my side and then back as we go down so as to reduce the force of impact, and we both roll on the ground, I silent and out of breath, he laughing, and the damned balloon somewhere high up, invisible to my eyes, I hold onto him, clutching him tightly, and say softly in an accusing voice, Sebastian, Sebastian, and he snuggles up to me, makes himself comfortable, and whispers into my ear, Do you want to hear a story? I say nothing but snuggle up to him and, holding him even more tightly absorb his words as if cuddling in his strong arms.

It's night, and Flamina has just fallen asleep when she hears the little bird go, Ping! on the windowsill of the open window, and she knows what it means, and is wide awake, and gets out of bed and sees the little bird fly away, and she walks up to the window and gets up on the windowsill , and steps out into the garden, and it's a moonlit night, and it's dark under the trees but the grass looks silver with dew where the moon is shining, and it feels cold and wet under Flamina's feet but she walks on and climbs over the little fence at the end of the garden, and the brook as always is purling there, and the little silver boat with the golden oar is waiting for her on its bank, and she pushes it in the water, and steps into it, and sits down, and starts rowing, and is carried quickly along, so she barely has to row, only directing the boat from time to time this way and that as it travels along the winding brook, and before she knows it she's in The Magic Sea, which looks like an enormous, giant, magnifying glass placed over a vast sunny landscape way underneath, with mountains and valleys, and forests, and fields, and roads cutting through them, and carts, and horses, and people on them, and villages, and towns along them with houses with steep red-tiled roofs, and churches with tall sharp spires in them along wide squares, and people gathered in them and walking in the streets, and way in the distance she can see a beautiful sail ship quietly waiting, and her boat immediately starts going toward the ship by itself, without her having to row or direct it, and before she knows it again, she is at the side of the ship, and a silk ladder with silver rungs is lowered over the side of the ship, and she steps onto one of the rungs, and climbs, and soon again finds herself on the deck where the boy Flamino is waiting for her, dressed in a loose white silk shirt with long puffy sleeves, and tight green satin pants and tall boots of yellow Moroccan leather, and at that moment she notices that her nightgown has turned into a long green satin dress, and there are soft golden slippers on her feet and a sheer white veil is draped over her head. They embrace, the sails of the ship fill up with wind like huge white swans, and Flamino's sleeves do too, looking like baby swans, like swanlings that follow big swans as they swim along, and the ship takes off toward a spot on the horizon, which gradually gets bigger and bigger, and which is The Magic Island they go to that always changes its shape like an overcoat thrown on the floor that manages to move around by itself. The little sliver boat with its golden oar is nowhere to be seen but it will be waiting for Flamina in the spot she left it in when the morning comes, and she and Flamino are ready to return to their homes.

There are good friends of Flamino and Flamina living on the island, four little gnomes called Romo, Roro, Momo, and Moro, and their friend, the brave little mushroom Ero, whose problem is that when he thinks hard his cap gets hot and starts steaming and he is in the danger of cooking himself. To prevent this, he has to be shaken violently so that he stops thinking, which is what the gnomes always do. And the five of them have a lot of thinking to do, since they fight a huge dragon called Blacktooth who lives on the island and *they want to find new ways of causing him trouble. Blacktooth feeds on coal and gets it by flying to the supermarket and brings it back in paper bags which he carries each stuck under one of his sixteen legs. Blacktooth locks the cave as he flies away and puts the key under a rock. The gnomes know which rock it is and sometimes get out the key, unlock the door, put the key back under the rock, hide, and laugh their heads off as they see Blacktooth get the key and lock the door when he gets back from shopping and tear the door out of its frame because he thinks he has unlocked it. He is very strong but very stupid. Blacktooth lives as long as there is fire burning in his belly and the way to harm him is to open the door at the bottom and shovel out the burning coal. Ero is helpful in this because he can get under Blacktooth's belly and open the door with his spear. When the fire is out of Blacktooth's belly his wife has to start it from scratch and bring her husband back to life. To help them fight Blacktooth as well as for other troubles, the gnomes have glass jars filled with time which, when they are opened, make everything stop except the gnomes and Ero. This is very helpful except there is a danger of time running out, so the gnomes have to be very fast while using the time jars. When the jars are empty, the gnomes refill them at the time spring which bubbles silently in a dark spot in the woods. Flamino and Flamina often watch the fights between the gnomes and Blacktooth, sitting at some distance on their horses with Flamina strumming her lute and describing in her singing voice what is going on.*

The gnomes are small but have big feet and as they are fond of dancing together, they step on each other's feet and yell, Stop it! and, Stop it! and, Stop it! and often wind up fighting each other by smacking their partner on the face. They live in a nice house and like to sleep at night with the windows open, and there is a person on the island who no one has seen called Someone. He likes to come sometimes in the middle of the night and digs a pit in the ground in which there are stairs leading to another world in which everything is upside down. The noise he makes while digging, Swoosh, swoosh, swoosh, makes the gnomes wake up in the order they are named, Romo through Moro, and as they sit up, except for Romo, each asks the preceding person, Who is it? and the person says, Someone, and in the end they know what is going on, and they rush out to catch Someone. But each time there is no one there and the gnomes can't resist opening the door at the bottom of the stairs and going into the upside-down world. They are a little disoriented at first when they get there because they are upside down, but soon get used to it and like being there a lot. The worlds down there are different in other ways too from ours, like with the sky and the sea being pink instead of blue and the leaves on the trees being purple. When the gnomes get back home, they feel disoriented too at first but get back to feeling normal soon. Once they come up to their place, the pit fills itself up by itself and there's never any sign of it having been there.

The Magic Island is ruled by The Good Fairy who lives in a big wonderful palace with many rooms, in which there are also worlds of different colors, like in the upside-down world. The Good Fairy throws many parties there and it is at these that the gnomes like to dance, which always ends up in shouting matches and face-slapping contests.

As the sail ship approaches the island, you can see The Good Fairy's palace high on the hill above the harbor with a beautiful formal garden stretching down from the front steps to the water. The sail ship docks by itself and as Flamino and Flamina get on the shore, there is The Good Fairy waiting for them with a retinue of servants and musicians and a pair of horses which are for Flamino and Flamina to ride on. She is dressed in a long blue satin dress and golden slippers on her feet and a tall golden conical hat from which drapes a sheer white veil that covers her face. She is tall and slender and beautiful, has golden hair, and her blue eyes sparkle like the diamond on the end of her magic wand which she always carries with her.

It is sunny and warm, the air is filled with a powerful scent of roses, the musicians strum their lutes and play their pipes, and the horses snort impatiently as they stand a little farther away, held by the horse grooms. The Good Fairy embraces Flamino and Flamina by kissing them on the cheeks and saying, Welcome to the magic island, children! and escorts them to the horses. The grooms help the two get up in the saddle, and after Flamina and Flamino say good-bye to The Good Fairy they ride off into the nearby woods. The horses know their way and walk by themselves along the wide, well-trodden path. It is shady and pleasantly cool in the woods, and the air is fraught with the scent of the cypress trees which grow all around. Soon the two find themselves in a clearing at the end of which stands a beautiful single-story cottage made of stone covered with a slate roof, partly hidden behind the tall rosebushes growing in the flower garden in front. Two or three servants can be seen standing by the open door ready to welcome their masters' home.

I drift off, lulled into sleep by his soft voice, safe in his strong arms.

29

MOTHER CARRIED THE child in a white moon and I held his hand as we walked through the night, now in blinding white moonlight in the clearings, now in an even more blinding black darkness under the huge, tall trees, along the path, along the white, trodden, clay path winding its way down the steep clayey slope toward the huge river below on the left, both of us naked, that is, both of us near-naked, I in plain linen trousers and shirt, he in his loose night shirt, all white, all items of clothing white, clutching, holding, that is, he clutching, holding in his right hand the string with the balloon on the end, the white balloon, tugging, pulling, that is, the balloon tugging, pulling skyward, moonward, like an animal, a pet, a dog on a leash trying to get to something, something to sniff or eat or just see, like a child, a son reaching out with his arms to his father, wanting to be picked up by him, to be held, to be one with him, the full moon in the sky, high up, in the zenith, looking like a giant white balloon, the white balloon on the end of his string like a baby moon, pulling, tugging on the string in order to be with his father, to be held by him, to be one with him, one with the huge white father-moon, down and down we trod, stepping carefully sometimes so as not to fall down, so as not to slip on the sometimes slippery, smooth, trodden, clay path, not to slip and fall down, his little hand, his left little hand, I think, yes, his hot left little hand tensing up at times, clutching more strongly, as strongly as it can, my right, my right one, asking for, getting support, down and down, we trod, sometimes nearly slipping, I nearly slipping, he always held up by my hand, shadows like huge black leaves, giant black leaves of a giant black maple tree falling over us, obscuring, blocking our vision, burying us completely as we make our way from one clearing in the bright moonlight to another, some big, other small, tiny, a mere chance to catch our visual breath, finally we're there, in a huge clearing, clearing of light and space, flat, bordered by trees, tall dense trees, now wait, a huge clearing bordered by trees? on the river? how would that be possible? no, not on the river, someplace else, still on the slope, the tall river bank, yes, no river this time, a crowd, a small crowd, a sizeable group of people gathered in the center, men and women, men and women only? no children? don't know, not sure, him at my side, yes, but children in the crowd? the group? not sure, probably not, probably for some reason not, probably just he, anyway, all, everyone dressed the same as we, white trousers and shirts, long shirts and dresses, all white, anyway again, we join, I and he join, join in, a ritual, the women in the center in a circle, facing each other, the men, we in a bigger circle around them facing them too, then straining, a lot of straining by the women, faces swollen, eyes popping out, groans, moans streaming, steaming out of partly or widely opened mouths, balloons being forced up under the loose shirts or dresses, up to the chin, the opening under the chin, some escaping, other still trying, desperately clambering upward toward the wished-for opening, she, his mother not far from us, from me and him, eyes skyward, way under the eyebrows, the eye socket bone, mouth open, twisted with the effort, nothing, nothing coming out, nothing seen to be pushing its way out, no balloon apparently, painful, very painful, very painful to watch, more balloons flying out, rising into the sky, streaming, their strings wiggling like the flagella on the end of sperms, spermatozoa, desperately heading toward the moon, their father, their giant father, like spermatozoa toward the egg they desperately want to impregnate, then less and less, fewer and fewer, soon

Yuriy Tarnawsky

there'll be none, nothing yet from her, from his mother, no sign, no hope this'll change, the expression on her face unbearable, excruciating, a crucifix, Christ on the cross, then something strange, unbelievable, he, my son at my side, my right side whose hand I'm clutching, starts rising, levitating, unsteady, swaying, getting lighter, feet obviously off the ground, rising higher and higher, higher and higher in my peripheral vision, in my right eye, I look, yes! my god! he's being pulled up by the balloon, carried up into the sky by the balloon, is about to join the balloons, be the last balloon in the cloud of them floating toward the moon, I hold his hand, my hand clutches his, keeps rising like a balloon, it's up to my shoulder, then above it, higher, on the level of my head, higher, I tug on it, it keeps pulling me up, I tug more, it keeps on pulling me up, it won't let him go, it wants to take my son away, wants to take him to the moon, to leave me alone, alone on this empty, lonely, forsaken earth, no! no! I can't permit it, can't let it happen! I mustn't let him go! the evil thing, the evil balloon, the evil flying serpent of a balloon! pretty soon my feet will be off the ground and I will lose my strength, will be like Antaeus, a modern-day Antaeus, won't be able to free him, free my son, will fall down sooner or later because I wouldn't be able to hold on to his hand all the way

244

up to the moon and he will go there by himself! I mobilize all my forces, feel my face strain, give one more tug, one last tug, the most powerful tug I ever gave, the most powerful tug I am able to give, having put all my strength, all my energy to the last erg or watt into it, emitting at the same time a loud, a deafening scream, and moan, and groan, and feel myself become free, feel him become free of the balloon, free of the damned balloon, feel him fall on top of me and then both of us fall to the ground, I clutching his precious body to mine with the vast flood of energy which has suddenly arisen in me as I hit the ground and wake up, I am clutching myself so hard, I hurt, an empty gray square stretches above my head, a gray square? the ceiling, yes, the ceiling, where am I? what's going on? where is everybody? where is somebody? Hello, hello! Hey! no answer, I am alone, as it sounds in a big empty space, a house most probably, a house, yes, my house, my home, yes, that's it, my home, for sure, I'm in my home, but where is everybody? where are they? Hey, hey! Hello! no answer, Hey! no answer, am I alone? permanently alone? abandoned? no, not possible, it couldn't be, I couldn't be living alone in the state I seem to be in, I wouldn't last, couldn't survive, would die of hunger, dehydration, desiccation, lack of care, I'm not living alone, I'm living with someone, a woman, I think, my wife, I think, yes, my wife most probably, my wife, yes, and maybe someone else, a man, a young man, my son, most probably, why most probably? why even probably? probably not, couples don't live with other people, with adults, any more, children, young children, yes, but adult children, no, not often, although you can't exclude that, you never know, and I'm too old to have a young son, a young son or daughter, so just a wife? I have just a wife? yes, most probably, although once again, you never know, you can't exclude anything, but a wife? yes, I have a wife, for sure, I live with my wife, she works to support us, to help us live better, to supplement my meager pension, yes, she's at work, should be home soon, should be home now, I think, it's late, the ceiling's dark, dark gray, almost black, she should be home, so where is she? why isn't she here? why hasn't she called to tell me she'll be late? why isn't she calling? has she abandoned me? walked out on me? Hey, hey! what's her name? I seem to have forgotten it, it's crazy to have forgotten your wife's name, but here you are, I've done it, A, A, A, I can't remember, can't remember her name, it must end in an "a," probably ends in an "a" as most female names do, I'll try that, it might help, Aaaa! Aaaa!

Aaaa! it doesn't, it doesn't help, using the ending of a person's name for calling doesn't help, doesn't work, she's not here, quiet, quiet, don't panic, nothing's lost yet, she couldn't have abandoned you, not so suddenly, not without a warning, without a reason, without giving you a chance, nothing's probably happened to her on the way home from work either, nothing happened, the road is straight, not winding, it's a divided highway, there're no trucks on it, there's just one tricky spot on it where the cars come in fast from the right and she has to turn off, turn off right soon afterwards, but she's aware of it, she's careful there, she's a good, a careful driver, she's alright, she just got delayed for some reason, something with her job, she has a lot of responsibility, she had to do something, she's alright, she'll be home soon, stay calm, don't panic, everything will be alright, everything will be fine, you must be patient, you must wait.

30

YOU CLIMB THE stairs of success, climb them each day, each day a step, each day a step up, a step closer to the top, one more and you'll be there, just one more step and you will have made it, one more, just one more, yes, just one more, yes, and finally you're there, finally you've made it, you've climbed that final, that last step and, in a cruel Escher trick, you're at the bottom landing with the stairs behind you which you can't climb again, a concrete wall on the right and left, and a door before you, a door which opens into nothing, into an empty space, a space without right or left, without top or bottom, and you must open it, must open that door and must step forward, and you will, he found himself on the landing July 28, July 28, 1750, courtesy of the charlatan John Taylor, a tailor by profession, I presume, a master of needle and thread, of scissors and cloth very likely, the John Taylor, who did in Handel nine years later, two of the greatest, yes, two of the greatest of all time, the greatest two out of three at the time, with Scarlatti, Domenico Scarlatti being the third, so two of the three greatest at the time, born thirty days and one hundred thirty kilometers apart, taken care of in one fell swoop, well, in two fell swoops nine years apart, but what's the difference? the same man and the identical effect, was buried in Johanniskirche on July 31, lost, found, reburied in 1894, then in St. Thomaskirche in 1949, where he had worked as cantor for twenty-seven years, left behind 1 share in a silver mine, 231 thaler in cash, medals, dishes, candle sticks, silverware, silver dagger, gold ring, 6 tables, 18 chairs, 7 beds, 11 shirts valued at 0 thaler, more, a herd of instruments, harpsichords, violins, violas, viola da gambas, 1 cello, I think, more, 52 sacred books, etc., etc. worth a total of 1122 thalers less 152 owed, that's how much? what's the grand total? wait, wait, no, I can't figure it out right now, can't calculate the number, less than a thousand, I think, yes, less than a thousand for sure, but I can't get the exact number, weird, it's weird, I remember all these numbers but can't calculate this simple difference, it's like earlier with the titles and numbers on the one hand and the facts and events of my life on the other, as I said, this means something, although I can't figure out right now what, it's maddening, I used to be so good at it, at numbers, at handling numbers, and can't calculate this simple subtraction now, wait, wait, let me try it one more time, 1100 minus 100 that's 1000, then 52 minus 22 that's 30, and 1000 minus 30 that's 970, got it! I got it! so it's 970, the grand total of his worth at death was 970, 970 thalers, but remember also the 1127 extant works, 1127! 142 CDs! 142! the output of ten busy composers, of twenty lazy ones, with many more of his works lost, lost beyond the 1127, and the children, don't forget the children, the twenty children, the twenty children he sired, ten of which survived and nine survived him, a volcano, a volcano of flesh, I mean life, a volcano of life and art, a master of intellect and soul, no one, there has been no one like him, no one ever, in the world, no artist or scientist, no artist for sure, ever, the greatest of all time, one of the greatest for sure, the greatest composer, yes, of course, but no artist to match him, to match him in form and feeling, he, the best in music, Michelangelo in art, and Shakespeare in literature? in the three genres, yes, very likely, but overall, no one to match him, Michelangelo never crossed the boundary of the visual, unmatched perhaps in the scope and craft but still just visual, Old Will? Old Will's great, he's great, of course, great in the letters, unmatched for sure, the greatest, unmatched in the language, in the poetry, and in characters, the characters he created, bore, sired, but plots? the plots?

dramatic tension, yes, terrific! but the results? seven corpses on the stage floor in Hamlet plus Hamlet himself!   that's eight, that's eight limp bodies on the dusty stage floorboards! that's very many, too many for my liking and for his, for Old Will's own good, and then this, O, my dear Hamlet! The drink, the drink! I'm poisoned! bad taste, bad taste like with Mozart and with the other one, the writer, I forget his name, don't feel obliged to remember it, not in the same league, of course, commercial interest, considerations, the public's taste, taste of the plebs on the benches in his case, I suspect, earned his bread writing plays, but look at the three Great Greeks, they also earned their bread writing plays, but it wasn't as commercial at the time, it's true, not as in the proto-capitalist Elizabethan England, so it's the age, the taste, commercial, financial considerations that must be the factor in his case, but still, bad taste, bad taste, yet on the other hand consider, Out, out, brief candle! Life's but a poor player that struts and frets his hour upon a lonely stage and then is heard no more. It is a tale told by an idiot, full of sound and fury, signifying nothing, wow! something like that, actually better, a bit better, but anyway, it's close enough, I could recall it word for word, but it's not necessary, it's good enough, it's true, but twenty? twenty children? no, not necessary, one standing in the doorway or cuddling you on the floor while telling you a story is enough, get off the stage, the empty stage, the blank sheet of paper, the empty canvas, the empty big silver or the small TV screen, step away from that piano that has opened its mouth wide and bared its huge teeth at you ready to devour you and multiply, be fruitful, as the good book says, be like a fruit fly.

DEAD STILL ALL around as in a tomb, am I in a tomb? dead? no, impossible, I'd be gasping, I mean, if I'm in a tomb, I'd be gasping if I were alive, otherwise I'd be dead, and I couldn't be dead because I'm thinking, you are, therefore you think, and if you think, you're alive, I don't believe in this crap of thinking in your grave, remembering, recollecting, it's not much better than "afterlife," sitting on a cloud and singing hymns to the Almighty, while bored angels mechanically strum their harps nearby, but where am I then that it's dead still all around as in a tomb? in a hospital? unlikely, there'd be equipment all over me, people around, I wouldn't be in a private room, don't warrant that, couldn't afford it, the stillness moreover feels different than in a single room, it's everywhere, all-penetrating, all-permeating, you don't have that kind of stillness in a hospital, there's something always going on there, people and all, I must be in a private house then most likely, my own, my home, why would I be lying in bed in somebody else's home? who would have me there? I have no friends, no real good friends who'd

put me up in case of something, and there must be
something with me, judging from the way I feel, something
serious, perhaps grave, I must be in my own home then,
almost certainly so, but where are the others, my wife,
children? I did have a wife and children, didn't I? everybody
does or almost everybody, it almost always depends on the
person, and I'm not the kind of person who wouldn't have a
family, I'm sure of that, I am a family kind of person, so I
should have a family, but where are they momentarily? on
an errand? unlikely, they wouldn't leave me all alone in the
state I'm in, I'm also sure of that, and it's not as if it's been
quiet in the house for just a few moments and the person
who's there will stir and all of a sudden you'll know you're not
alone, it's been still like this for a while, for a long time in fact,
it's that kind of stillness, you can tell it by hearing it, it sounds
different, so where are they all? did they all die? I seem to
have attended a funeral recently, in fact I seem to have just
returned from a funeral, but whose funeral? my wife's? one
of my children's? all of them? that's unlikely, why unlikely?
it's quite possible, in fact it's quite likely, happens all the time
nowadays, a car accident or an act of terror, we were
together, driving in a car or attending some event and were
in a car crash or became victims of a terrorist attack

respectively, all were hurt, the others died, and I am the only survivor, but no, that's not it, for one, I wouldn't be at home all alone and I'd feel different, bereaved and so on, but the feeling I have is not like that, not bereaved, but abandoned, all alone, abandoned on purpose, by design, according to plan, so there's something else going on here, still there was a funeral, I'm sure, in driving rain, on a hill, the coffin on a horse-drawn wagon or in a hearse, a car hearse, I mean, a black automobile hearse, shiny from the rain, wet, slippery, blinding-green grass underfoot so that I had to lean to one side, left, I think, yes, left, in order not to slide down and fall, dug the edges of my shoes into the ground to make sure, were all muddy when I got home and I had to wash them in the sink in the bathroom, had a kink in my side the next day for a week or two because of that, no, not because of leaning, because of getting wet on that side from the rain and getting a chill, yes, that's right, it was my right side, the one that was exposed to the rain because I was leaning to the left, tried to hide under a huge umbrella, big as the sky, as the vast black sky overhead, above it, but wasn't quite able to, the rain kept coming in, the umbrella, big as it was, strangely enough wasn't big enough, not big enough even though as big as the vast black sky overhead, the sky somehow bigger, the rain somehow managing to get under the umbrella, and the sky blacker even though the umbrella as black as the sky, no umbrella could be as black as the sky if you're attending a funeral, the sky black not from the clouds, the rain, but from the funeral, but I probably didn't have a kink just because of the umbrella being too small and my getting wet on one side either but because of both, because of both leaning and being wet, but that's another matter, but who was the funeral for? who had died? there was only one coffin, I am sure, I remember seeing it pitifully small and lonely, small and abandoned, on that wagon, or inside the hearse, no, it was a wagon after all, a simple horse-drawn wagon, pulled by one horse, one miserable-looking skinny old horse, and there was one coffin on it, so it must have been one person, one person who had died, who could it have been? my wife? a child? it wasn't a woman though, wife, or daughter, I know that, it was a man, so it could have been a son, I must have had one, yes, I remember now, I did, what was/is his name? wait, wait a second, it's on the tip of my tongue, wait, wait, no, I can't remember it right now, won't remember it anytime soon either, not in the state I'm in, not with the way I feel, but it'll come back, I'm sure, I just have to be patient and it'll come back, so the funeral could have been for him and I was the only one there, the only mourner in addition to the gravedigger or gravediggers and the driver of the wagon or the hearse, don't remember how many, but why was I alone? where was my wife, his mother? I must have had a wife or a woman to have him with, and he of course did have a mother, did she die before him? no, I'm sure of that, I would have felt it then and would feel it now, but I don't know where she was, busy? what do I mean busy? how can you be too busy with something so that you wouldn't be able to attend your son's funeral? well, she may have been away, someplace far away on business and couldn't make it back in time, so I had to bury him alone, or maybe she abandoned him, abandoned both of us long time ago and didn't care what happened to him, hadn't been in touch with us for years, since his birth perhaps, or I didn't know how, or didn't want to get in touch with her to let her know our son had died because she had abandoned him and me long time ago, there could have been all sorts of reasons, anyway, there was no woman with me and I was there alone for the man who died, who may have been my son, but was it my son? I am not sure, that it was a man, I am sure, yes, but my son, no, not sure of that, so who could it have been? a friend? no,

Yuriy Tarnawsky

it wasn't a friend, it was someone very close to me, related, a brother? no, I never had a brother, an uncle, a relative? no, definitely not, it was someone very close, very, very close, as close as anybody can be, a son or father, so if it wasn't my son, then it must have been my father, yes, of course, it was my father, I remember now clearly, it was his funeral, we were the only two left of our family and when he died, I was the only one left to mourn him, it was some years ago though, I was still young then, but no, my father's funeral was different, there were many cars there, black, limousines, a flag leaning, grazing like a horse on the shiny funeral home tiled floor, and many people, I did have siblings, a brother and a sister, I remember now, and they were there, yes, for sure, so this was a different funeral, different from the one I've just attended, I'm all confused, was I actually at such a funeral as I've described? I'm not sure now, it's possible I'm just imagining, I may have read about it someplace and think now that it was I who attended it, by association, being in a similar situation, putting myself in that person's, the mourner's place, yes, I think so, it's quite possible that this is what happened, in fact I am almost sure now that that's what happened, that I have read someplace about such a funeral and in the state I'm in confused it with what I've lived through, probably through association, being in a similar situation, putting myself in that person's, the mourner's place, so it also means that I didn't attend any funeral recently as I have thought earlier, that I'm just back from one, which most likely means that my son hasn't died because I surely would remember it even in the state I'm in, the way I feel, that is, if I had him, if I ever had a son, but I must have had one, why would I have been punished in such a horrible way as to have been denied the gift of having a son? I hadn't done anything to deserve it, fate couldn't have been so cruel as to deny me that natural gift, so I probably have one and he's just away, went out on an errand, to do something important, to get something, for instance for himself, or for us both, medicine or food, or a special kind of drink, an electrolyte drink for me for instance, or for both of us, and will be back soon to attend to me, I must be patient, I must wait.

Georg Trakl

SEBASTIAN IM TRAUM

Translated by Yuriy Tarnawsky

Sebastian im Traum

Für Adolf Loos

1.

Mutter trug das Kindlein im weißen Mond,
Im Schatten des Nußbaums, uralten Holunders,
Trunken vom Safte des Mohns, der Klage der
    Drossel;
Und stille
Neigte in Mitleid sich über jene ein bärtiges Antlitz

Leise im Dunkel des Fensters; und altes
    Hausgerät
Der Väter
Lag im Verfall; Liebe und herbstliche Träumerei.

Also dunkel der Tag des Jahrs, traurige Kindheit,
Da der Knabe leise zu kühlen Wassern, silbernen
    Fischen hinabstieg,
Ruh und Antlitz;
Da er steinern sich vor rasende Rappen warf,
In grauer Nacht sein Stern über ihn kam;

Oder wenn er an der frierenden Hand der Mutter
Abends über Sankt Peters herbstlichen Friedhof
    ging,
Ein zarter Leichnam stille im Dunkel der Kammer
    lag
Und jener die kalten Lider über ihn aufhob.

Er aber war ein kleiner Vogel im kahlen Geäst,
Die Glocke lang im Abendnovember,
Des Vaters Stille, da er im Schlaf die dämmernde
    Wendeltreppe hinabstieg

Sebastian in a Dream

For Adolf Loos

1.

Mother carried the child in a white moon,
In the shadow of the walnut tree, of the age-old
    elderberry bush,
Drunk with the juice of poppies, with the complaint
    of the thrush;
And silently
A bearded face leaned over her with compassion

Quietly in the darkness of the window; and the old
    household things
Of the forefathers
Lay in decay; love and dreams of autumn.

So, dark the day of the year, a sad childhood,
Since the boy went down to cool waters, to silver
    fishes,
Peace and a face;
Because he threw himself stonelike before the
    galloping horses,
In the gray night his star rose above him;

Or when with his mother's ice-cold hand in his
He walked in the evening through the autumn
    cemetery of St. Peter's,
A gentle corpse lay in the darkness of the
    chamber
And it raised its cold eyelids over him.

But he was a tiny bird among bare branches,
The bell long in the evening November,
His father's stillness, since in his sleep he came
    down the dusky winding staircase.

2.

Frieden der Seele. Einsamer Winterabend,
Die dunklen Gestalten der Hirten am alten
    Weiher;
Kindlein in der Hütte von Stroh; o wie leise
Sank in schwarzem Fieber das Antlitz hin.
Heilige Nacht.

Oder wenn er an der harten Hand des Vaters
Stille den finstern Kalvarienberg hinanstieg
Und in dämmernden Felsennischen
Die blaue Gestalt des Menschen durch seine
    Legende ging,
Aus der Wunde unter dem Herzen purpurn das
    Blut rann.
O wie leise stand in dunkler Seele das Kreuz auf.

Liebe; da in schwarzen Winkeln der Schnee
    schmolz,
Ein blaues Lüftchen sich heiter im alten Holunder
    fing,
In dem Schattengewölbe des Nußbaums;
Und dem Knaben leise sein rosiger Engel
    erschien.

Freude; da in kühlen Zimmern eine Abendsonate
    erklang,
Im braunen Holzgebälk
Ein blauer Falter aus der silbernen Puppe kroch.

O die Nähe des Todes. In steinerner Mauer
Neigte sich ein gelbes Haupt, schweigend das
    Kind,
Da in jenem März der Mond verfiel.

2.

Peace of the soul, a lonely winter evening,
Dark shadows of herdsmen at the old pond;
A child in a straw hut; oh, how quietly
Sank into black fever the face.
Holy Night.

Or when with his father's hard hand in his
He walked silently down the dark Calvary
    Mountain
And in the twilight cliff niches
The blue figure of man walked through his legend,
From the wound under the heart the blood ran
    purply,
Oh, how quietly the cross rose up in the dark soul.

Love; since snow melted in black corners,
A blue breeze cheerfully got caught in the old
    elderberry bush,
In the shadow vault of the walnut tree;
And the boy's rose-colored angel silently
    appeared before him.

Joy; because in the cool rooms echoed the
    evening sonata,
In the brown wooden beams
A blue moth crept out of the silver pupa.

Oh, the nearness of death. In the stone walls
A yellow head leaned down, silencing the child,
Since that March the moon had waned.

3.

Rosige Oster Glocke im Grabgewölbe der Nacht
Und die Silberstimmen der Sterne,
Daß in Schauern ein dunkler Wahnsinn von der
    Stirne des Schläfers sank.

O wie stille ein Gang den blauen Fluß hinab
Vergessenes sinnend, da im grünen Geäst
Die Drossel ein Fremdes in den Untergang rief.

Oder wenn er an der knöchernen Hand des
    Greisen
Abends vor die verfallene Mauer der Stadt ging
Und jener in schwarzem Mantel ein rosiges
    Kindlein trug,
Im Schatten des Nußbaums der Geist des Bösen
    erschien.

Tasten über die grünen Stufen des Sommers. O
    wie leise
Verfiel der Garten in der braunen Stille des
    Herbstes,
Duft und Schwermut des alten Holunders,
Da in Sebastians Schatten die Silberstimme des
    Engels erstarb.

3.

Rosy Easter Bell in the tomb vault of the night
And the silver voices of the stars,
That in shudders a dark madness sank from the
    sleeper's forehead.
.
Oh, how still the walk down the blue river
Thinking about the forgotten, since in the green
    branches
The thrush called a strange one to doom.

Or when he with the bony hand of the old man in
    his
Walked in the evening along the crumbling wall of
      the city
And the former in a black cloak caried a rose-
    colored child,
In the shadow of the walnut tree appeared the
    spirit of evil.

Groping over the green steps of the summer. Oh,
    how peacefully
The garden withered away in the brown stillness
    of the autumn,
Fragrance and melancholy of the old elderberry
    bush,
Because in Sebastian's shadow died the silver
    voice of the angel.

Checklist of Previous JEF Titles